Disney
FAIRIES

Tinke

AND THE PIRAT



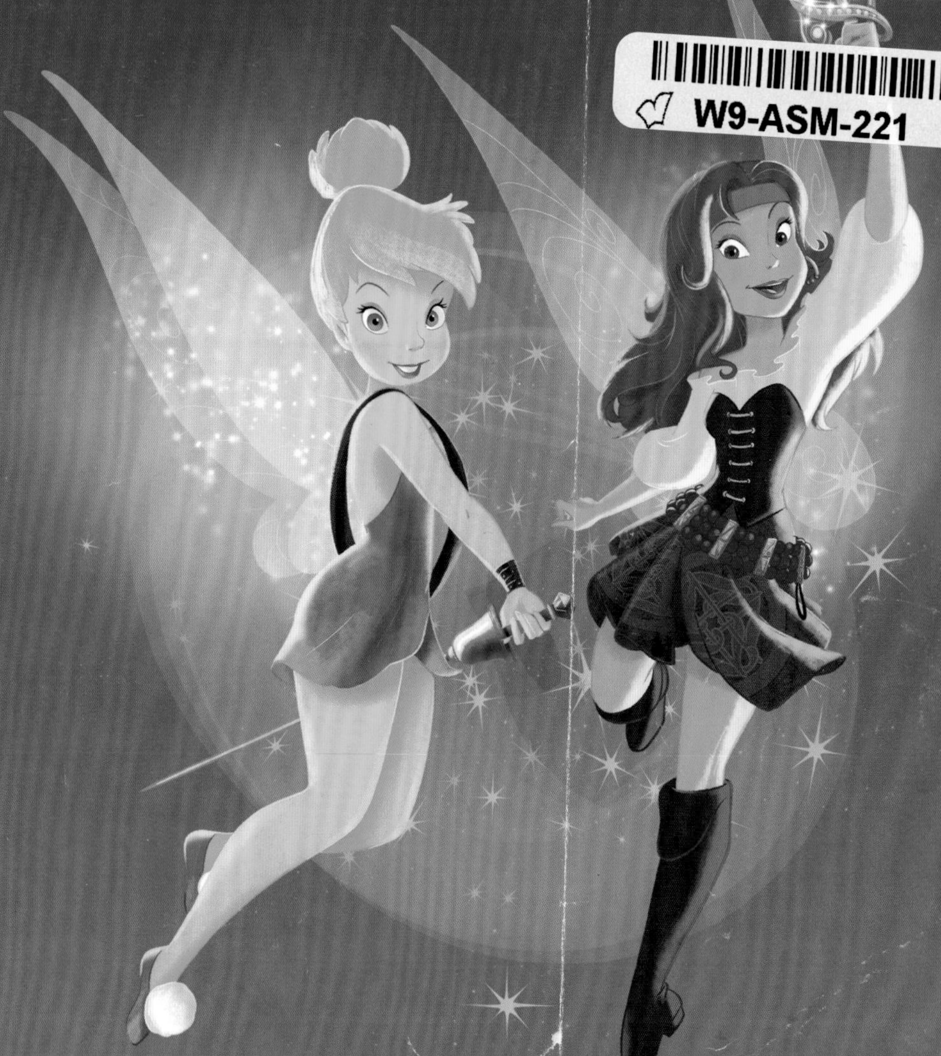

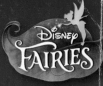

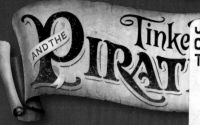

PAPERCUTZ™

# Graphic Novels Available from
## PAPERCUTZ

**Graphic Novel #1**
"Prilla's Talent"

**Graphic Novel #2**
"Tinker Bell and the Wings of Rani"

**Graphic Novel #3**
"Tinker Bell and the Day of the Dragon"

**Graphic Novel #4**
"Tinker Bell to the Rescue"

**Graphic Novel #5**
"Tinker Bell and the Pirate Adventure"

**Graphic Novel #6**
"A Present for Tinker Bell"

**Graphic Novel #7**
"Tinker Bell the Perfect Fairy"

**Graphic Novel #8**
"Tinker Bell and her Stories for a Rainy Day"

**Graphic Novel #9**
"Tinker Bell and her Magical Arrival"

**Graphic Novel #10**
"Tinker Bell and the Lucky Rainbow"

**Graphic Novel #11**
"Tinker Bell and the Most Precious Gift"

**Graphic Novel #12**
"Tinker Bell and the Lost Treasure"

**Graphic Novel #13**
"Tinker Bell and the Pixie Hollow Games"

**Graphic Novel #14**
"Tinker Bell and Blaze"

**Tinker Bell and the Great Fairy Rescue**

---

DISNEY FAIRIES graphic novels are available in paperback for $7.99 each;
in hardcover for $12.99 each except #5, $6.99PB, $10.99HC. #6-14 are $7.99PB $11.99HC.
Tinker Bell and the Great Fairy Rescue is $9.99 in hardcover only.
Available at booksellers everywhere.

## See more at papercutz.com

Or you can order from us: Please add $4.00 for postage and handling for first book, and add $1.00 for each
additional book. Please make check payable to NBM Publishing. Send to: Papercutz, 160 Broadway, Suite
700, East Wing, New York, NY 10038 or call 800 886 1223 (9-6 EST M-F) MC-Visa-Amex accepted.

**Graphic Novel #15**
"Tinker Bell and the Secret of the Wings"

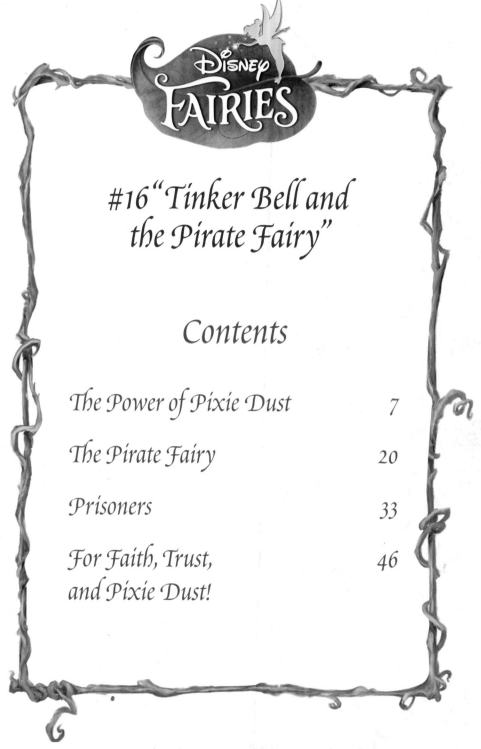

# #16 "Tinker Bell and the Pirate Fairy"

## Contents

PAPERCUTZ™

NEW YORK

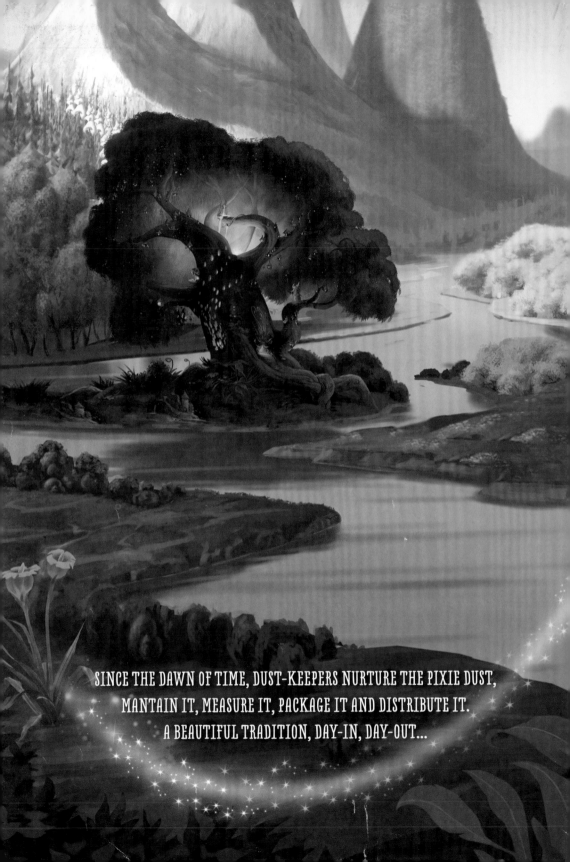

SINCE THE DAWN OF TIME, DUST-KEEPERS NURTURE THE PIXIE DUST,
MANTAIN IT, MEASURE IT, PACKAGE IT AND DISTRIBUTE IT.
A BEAUTIFUL TRADITION, DAY-IN, DAY-OUT...

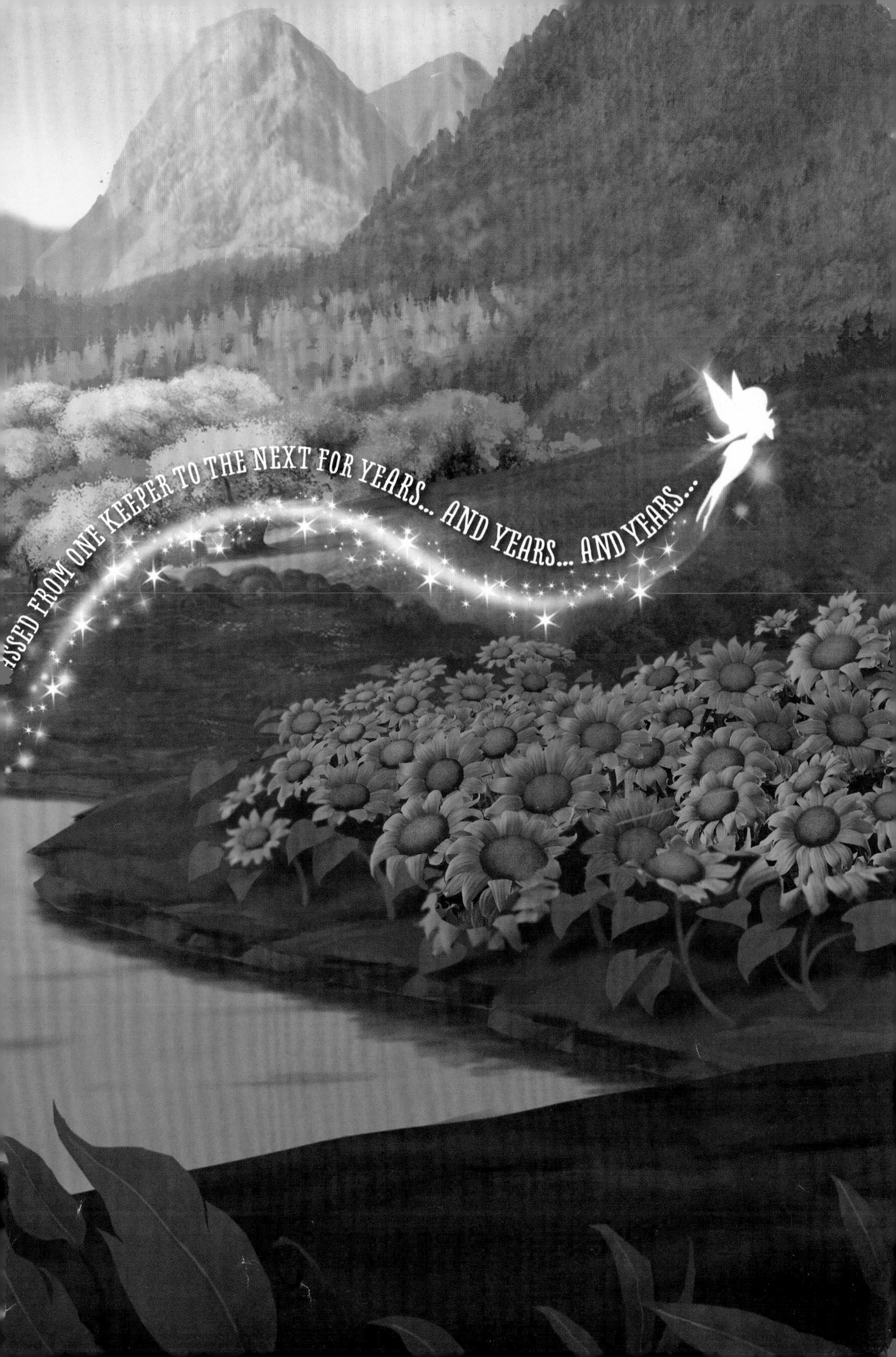
ASSED FROM ONE KEEPER TO THE NEXT FOR YEARS... AND YEARS... AND YEARS....

**"Tinker Bell and the Pirate Fairy"**
Script: Tea Orsi
(Based on the screenplay by Jeffrey M. Howard, Ryan Rowe, and Kate Kondell.)
Revised Captions: Cortney Faye Powell and Jim Salicrup
Layout: Andrea Greppi, Sara Storino, Emilio Urbano
Clean Up: Andrea Greppi, Manueala Razzi, Sara Storino
Inks: Michela Frare
Paint: Marieke Ferrari, Andrew Phillipson
Additional Art : Gianfranco Florio, Rosa LaBarbera, Francesco Legramandi,
Charles Pickens, John Raymond, Brian Sebern, Jeffrey Thomas, Lori Tyminski.

Production – Dawn K. Guzzo
Special Thanks – Krista Wong
Production Coordinator – Jeff Whitman
Associate Editor – Michael Petranek
Jim Salicrup
Editor-in-Chief

ISBN: 978-1-62991-153-3 paperback edition
ISBN: 978-1-62991-154-0 hardcover edition

Printed in China
February 2015 by Asia One Printing LTD
13/F Asia One Tower
8 Fung Yip St., Chaiwan
Hong Kong

Papercutz books may be purchased for business or promotional use. For information on bulk purchases please contact
Macmillan Corporate and Premium Sales Department at (800) 221-7945 x5442.

Distributed by Macmillan
First Papercutz Printing

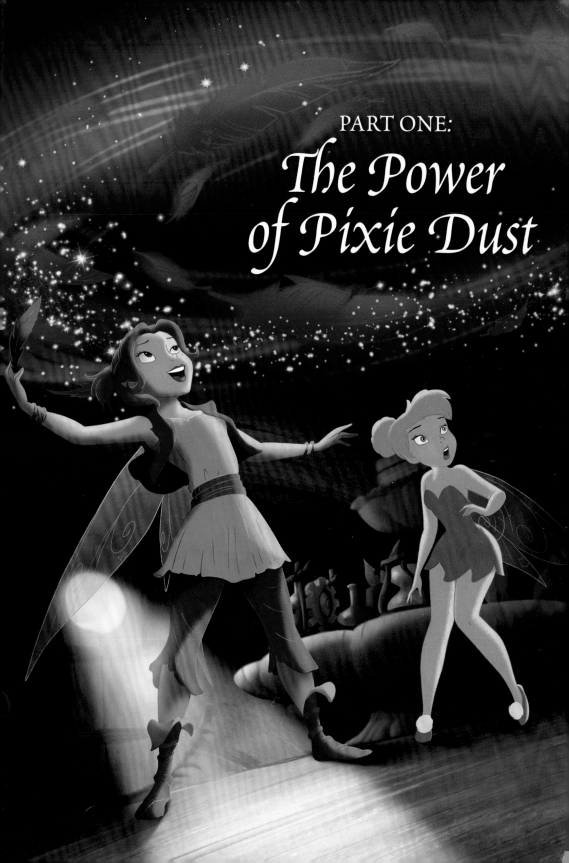

PART ONE:

# The Power of Pixie Dust

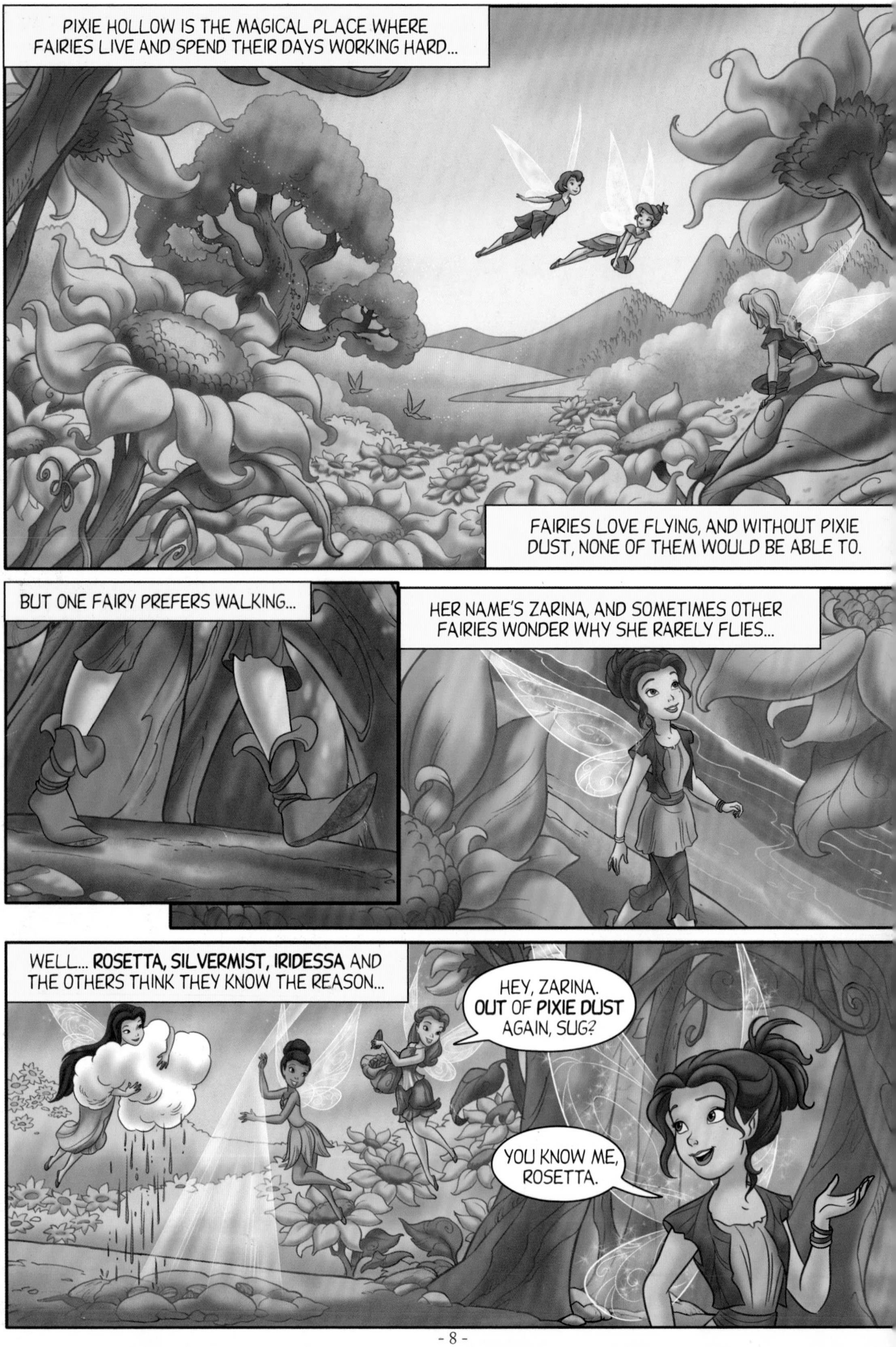
PIXIE HOLLOW IS THE MAGICAL PLACE WHERE FAIRIES LIVE AND SPEND THEIR DAYS WORKING HARD...
FAIRIES LOVE FLYING, AND WITHOUT PIXIE DUST, NONE OF THEM WOULD BE ABLE TO.
BUT ONE FAIRY PREFERS WALKING...
HER NAME'S ZARINA, AND SOMETIMES OTHER FAIRIES WONDER WHY SHE RARELY FLIES...
WELL... **ROSETTA, SILVERMIST, IRIDESSA** AND THE OTHERS THINK THEY KNOW THE REASON...
HEY, ZARINA. **OUT** OF **PIXIE DUST** AGAIN, SUG?
YOU KNOW ME, ROSETTA.

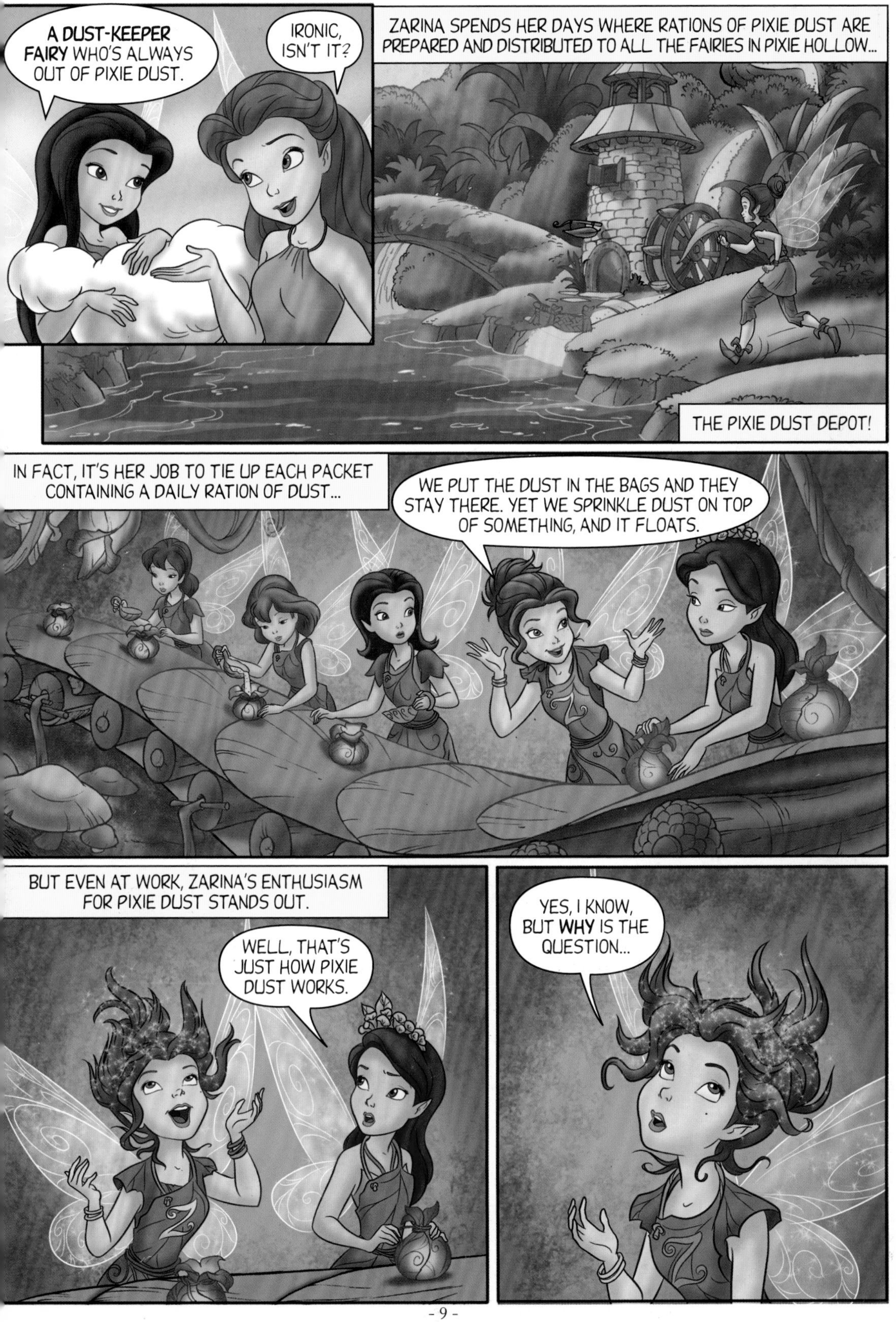
A **DUST-KEEPER FAIRY** WHO'S ALWAYS OUT OF PIXIE DUST.
IRONIC, ISN'T IT?
ZARINA SPENDS HER DAYS WHERE RATIONS OF PIXIE DUST ARE PREPARED AND DISTRIBUTED TO ALL THE FAIRIES IN PIXIE HOLLOW...
THE PIXIE DUST DEPOT!
IN FACT, IT'S HER JOB TO TIE UP EACH PACKET CONTAINING A DAILY RATION OF DUST...
WE PUT THE DUST IN THE BAGS AND THEY STAY THERE. YET WE SPRINKLE DUST ON TOP OF SOMETHING, AND IT FLOATS.
BUT EVEN AT WORK, ZARINA'S ENTHUSIASM FOR PIXIE DUST STANDS OUT.
WELL, THAT'S JUST HOW PIXIE DUST WORKS.
YES, I KNOW, BUT **WHY** IS THE QUESTION...

WHEN IT'S HER TURN TO ENTER THE **BLUE PIXIE DUST VAULT** WITH FAIRY GARY, ZARINA'S CURIOSITY IS AROUSED...

DOES THIS PLACE EVER LOSE ITS MAGIC?

UHH, SIX CLICKS TO THE RIGHT...

YES... THANK YOU!

TICK

TICK

THE BLUE PIXIE DUST IS THE MOST PRECIOUS, AND POWERFUL, PIXIE DUST OF ALL.

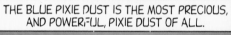

ALRIGHT THEN, EXACTLY **26 SPECKS**!

WHY NOT 25? WHAT WOULD HAPPEN IF WE PUT IN, SAY, 27?

ZARINA, YOU'RE THE MOST **INQUISITIVE** FAIRY I'VE EVER KNOWN. LET'S JUST SAY YOU'RE THE TINKER BELL OF DUST-KEEPERS.

BUT WHY DO YOU SAY THAT LIKE IT'S A BAD THING?

BECAUSE WE DON'T WORK WITH TWIGS AND ACORN CAPS. WE WORK WITH PIXIE DUST. IT'S OUR **LIFEBLOOD**. THERE'S NO ROOM FOR ERROR.

SIGH.

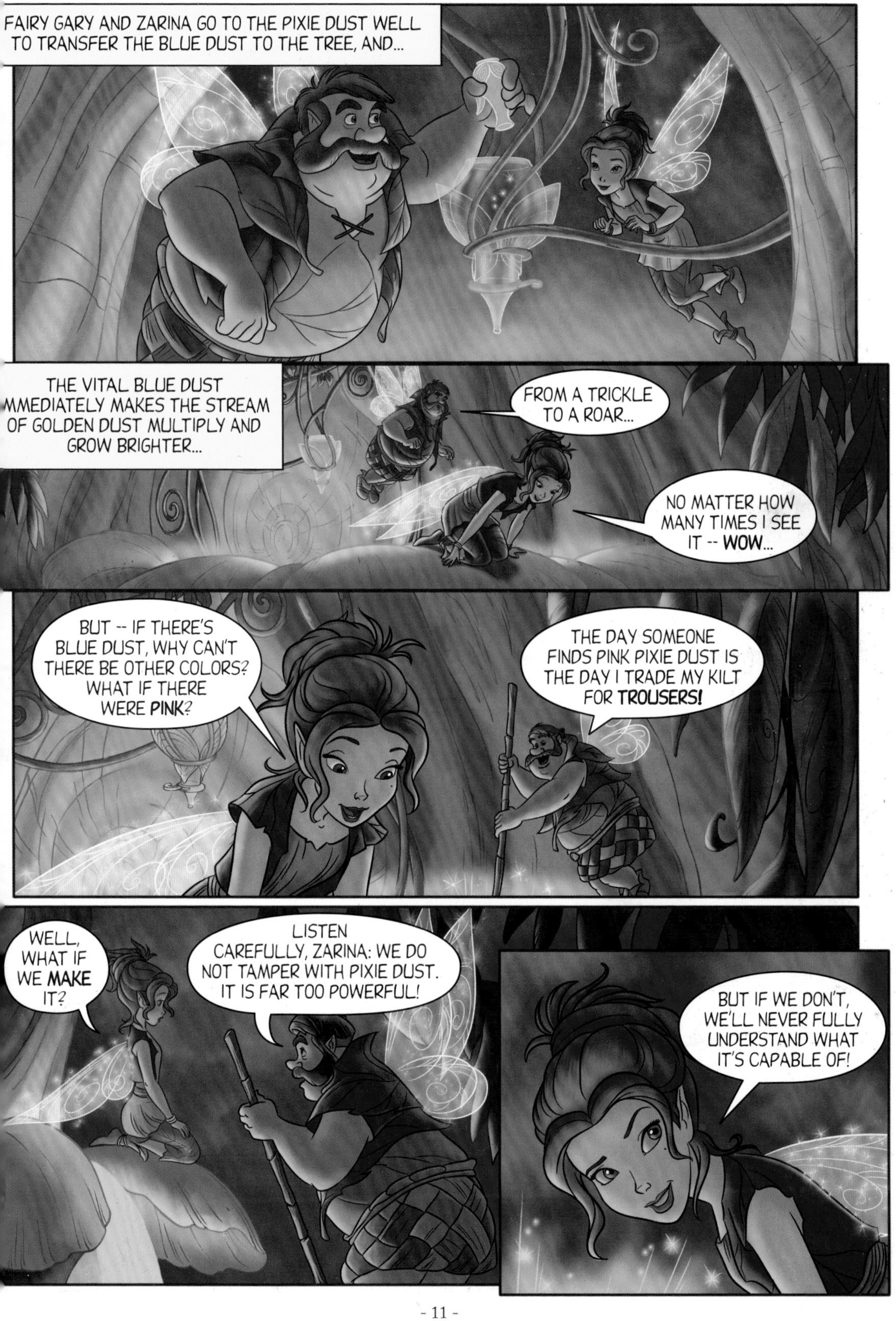
FAIRY GARY AND ZARINA GO TO THE PIXIE DUST WELL TO TRANSFER THE BLUE DUST TO THE TREE, AND...
THE VITAL BLUE DUST IMMEDIATELY MAKES THE STREAM OF GOLDEN DUST MULTIPLY AND GROW BRIGHTER...
FROM A TRICKLE TO A ROAR...
NO MATTER HOW MANY TIMES I SEE IT -- **WOW**...
BUT -- IF THERE'S BLUE DUST, WHY CAN'T THERE BE OTHER COLORS? WHAT IF THERE WERE **PINK**?
THE DAY SOMEONE FINDS PINK PIXIE DUST IS THE DAY I TRADE MY KILT FOR **TROUSERS!**
WELL, WHAT IF WE **MAKE** IT?
LISTEN CAREFULLY, ZARINA: WE DO NOT TAMPER WITH PIXIE DUST. IT IS FAR TOO POWERFUL!
BUT IF WE DON'T, WE'LL NEVER FULLY UNDERSTAND WHAT IT'S CAPABLE OF!

ZARINA'S CURIOUS, AND WHEN FAIRY GARY IS DISTRACTED...

THAT IS NOT OUR JOB. WE'RE DUST-KEEPERS!

... SHE CAN'T STOP HERSELF FROM EXPERIMENTING...

PLOP

WE **NURTURE** THE DUST, MAINTAIN IT, PACKAGE IT...

WHOOSH

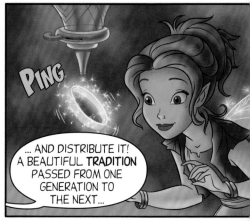

PING

... AND DISTRIBUTE IT! A BEAUTIFUL **TRADITION** PASSED FROM ONE GENERATION TO THE NEXT...

BUT WHEN A SINGLE SPECK OF BLUE DUST MEETS THE GOLDEN DUST ON THE BRACELET...

CLINK

...THE GOLDEN DUST PROLIFERATES AND...

BOING

GASP!

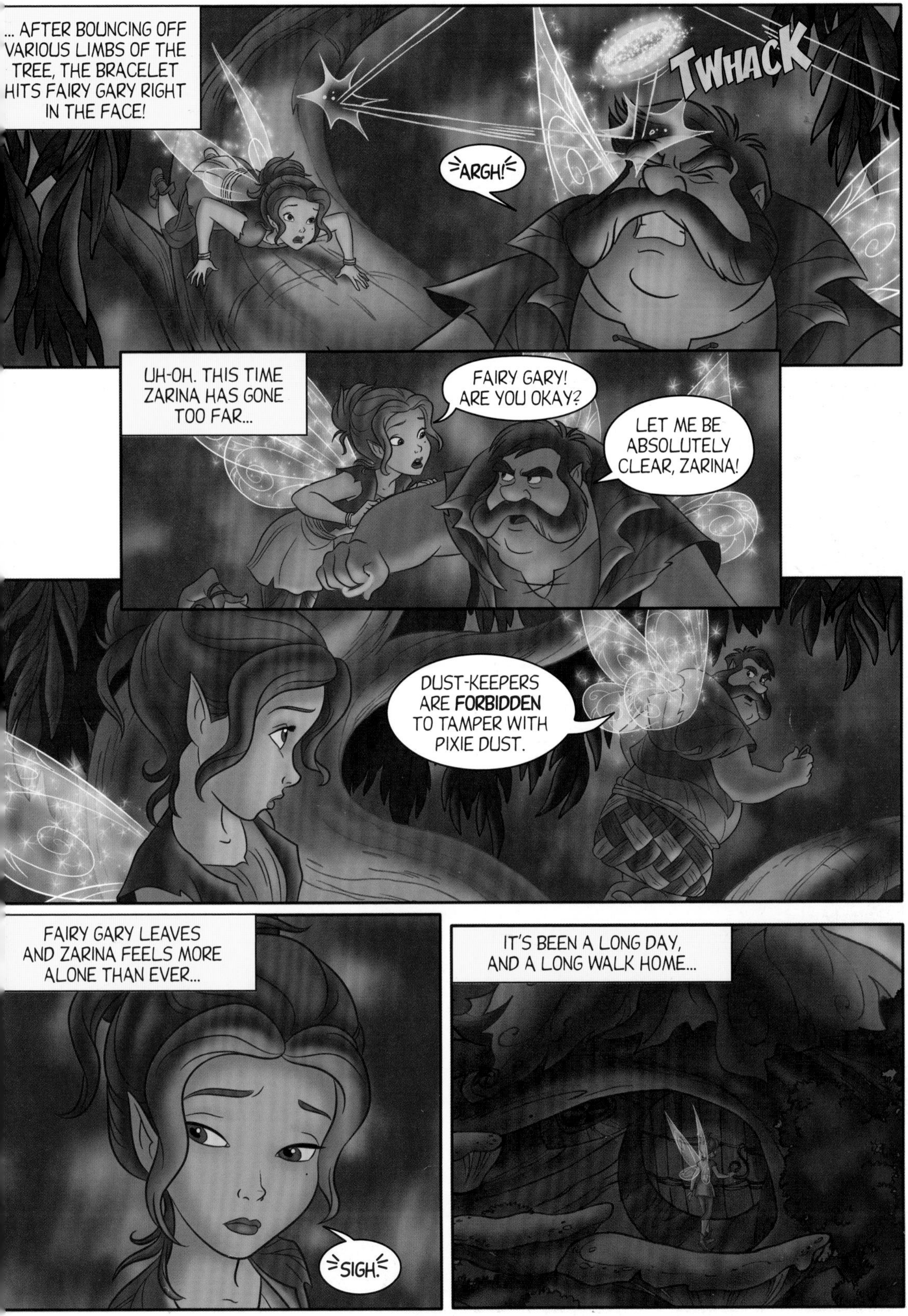
... AFTER BOUNCING OFF VARIOUS LIMBS OF THE TREE, THE BRACELET HITS FAIRY GARY RIGHT IN THE FACE!
TWHACK
ARGH!
UH-OH. THIS TIME ZARINA HAS GONE TOO FAR...
FAIRY GARY! ARE YOU OKAY?
LET ME BE ABSOLUTELY CLEAR, ZARINA!
DUST-KEEPERS ARE **FORBIDDEN** TO TAMPER WITH PIXIE DUST.
FAIRY GARY LEAVES AND ZARINA FEELS MORE ALONE THAN EVER...
SIGH.
IT'S BEEN A LONG DAY, AND A LONG WALK HOME...

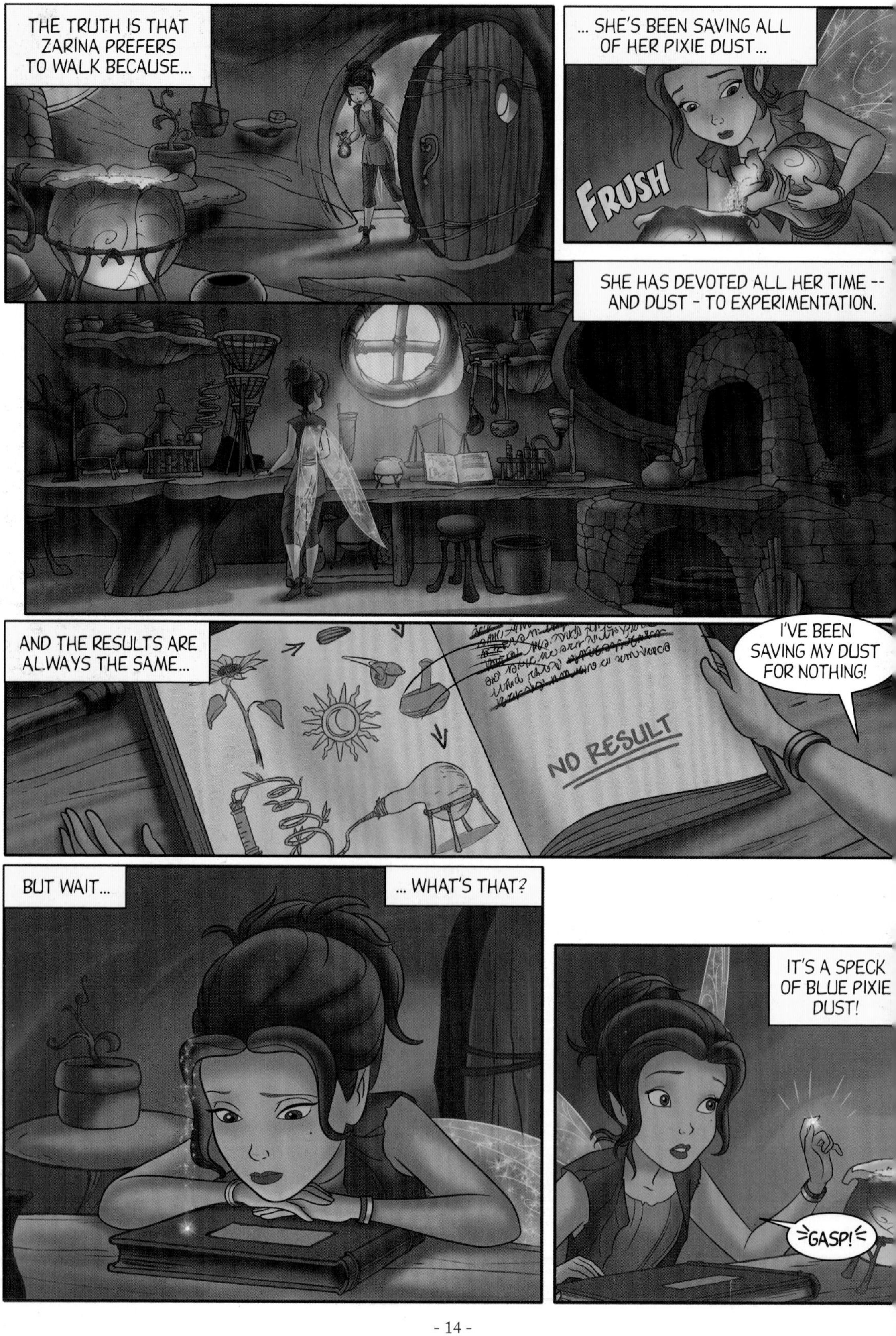
THE TRUTH IS THAT ZARINA PREFERS TO WALK BECAUSE...
... SHE'S BEEN SAVING ALL OF HER PIXIE DUST...
FRUSH
SHE HAS DEVOTED ALL HER TIME -- AND DUST - TO EXPERIMENTATION.
AND THE RESULTS ARE ALWAYS THE SAME...
NO RESULT
I'VE BEEN SAVING MY DUST FOR NOTHING!
BUT WAIT...
... WHAT'S THAT?
IT'S A SPECK OF BLUE PIXIE DUST!
GASP!

AND IT GIVES HER A GREAT IDEA...

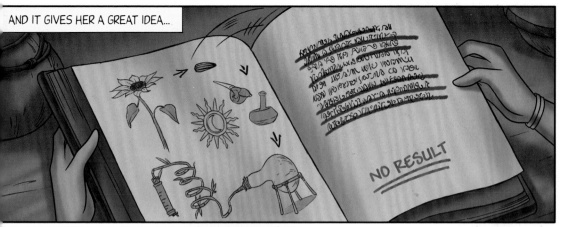

T'S TIME TO REPEAT A PREVIOUSLY FAILED EXPERIMENT...

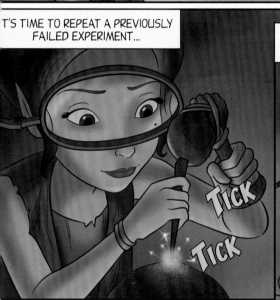

TICK

TICK

BUT THIS TIME ZARINA ADDS A TINY SLIVER OF BLUE DUST...

AND THE RESULT DOESN'T DISAPPOINT HER AT ALL...

HUH?

THE PIXIE DUST HAS DEFINITELY TURNED **ORANGE!**

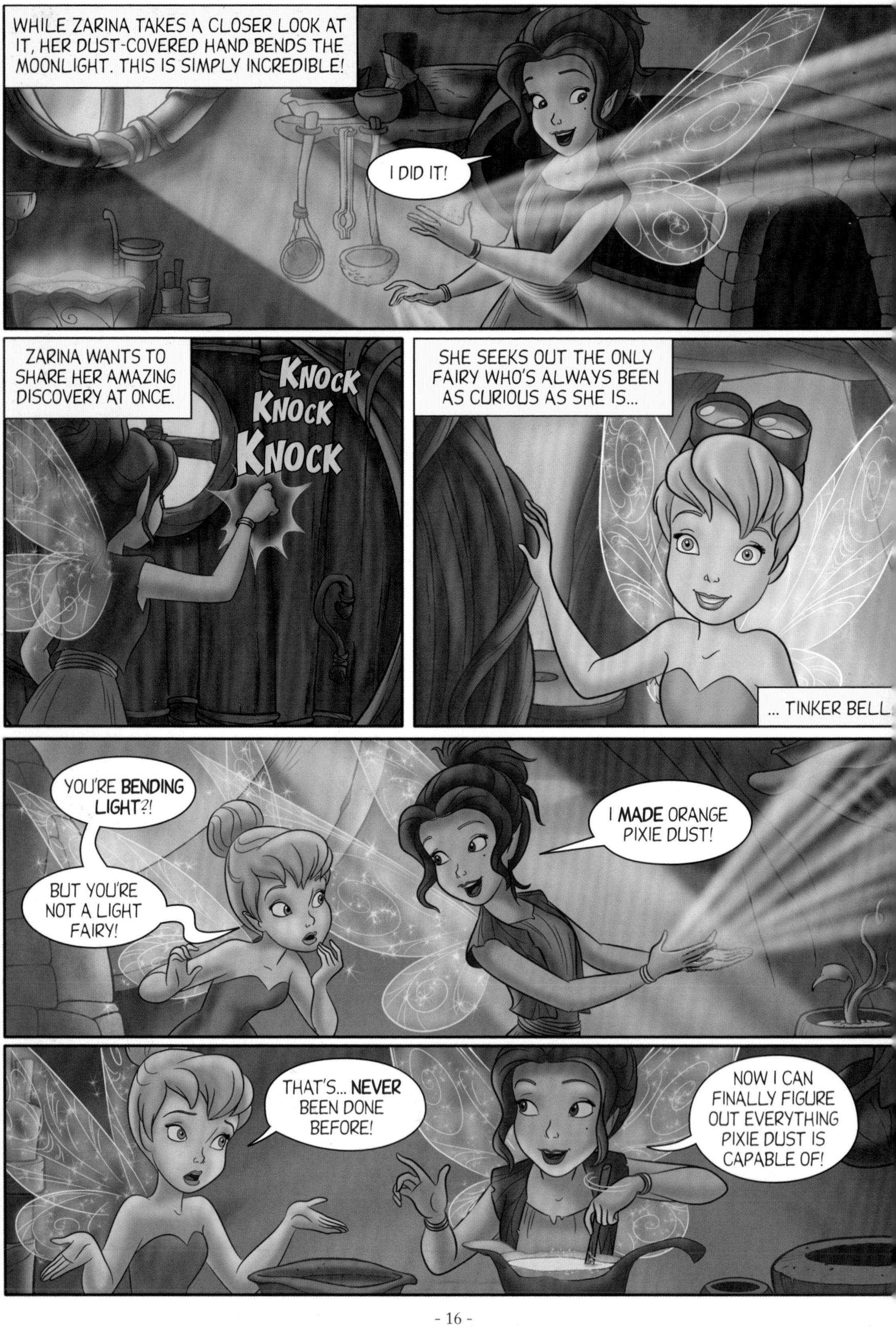
WHILE ZARINA TAKES A CLOSER LOOK AT IT, HER DUST-COVERED HAND BENDS THE MOONLIGHT. THIS IS SIMPLY INCREDIBLE!
I DID IT!
ZARINA WANTS TO SHARE HER AMAZING DISCOVERY AT ONCE.
KNOCK
KNOCK
KNOCK
SHE SEEKS OUT THE ONLY FAIRY WHO'S ALWAYS BEEN AS CURIOUS AS SHE IS...
... TINKER BELL.
YOU'RE BENDING LIGHT?!
BUT YOU'RE NOT A LIGHT FAIRY!
I MADE ORANGE PIXIE DUST!
THAT'S... NEVER BEEN DONE BEFORE!
NOW I CAN FINALLY FIGURE OUT EVERYTHING PIXIE DUST IS CAPABLE OF!

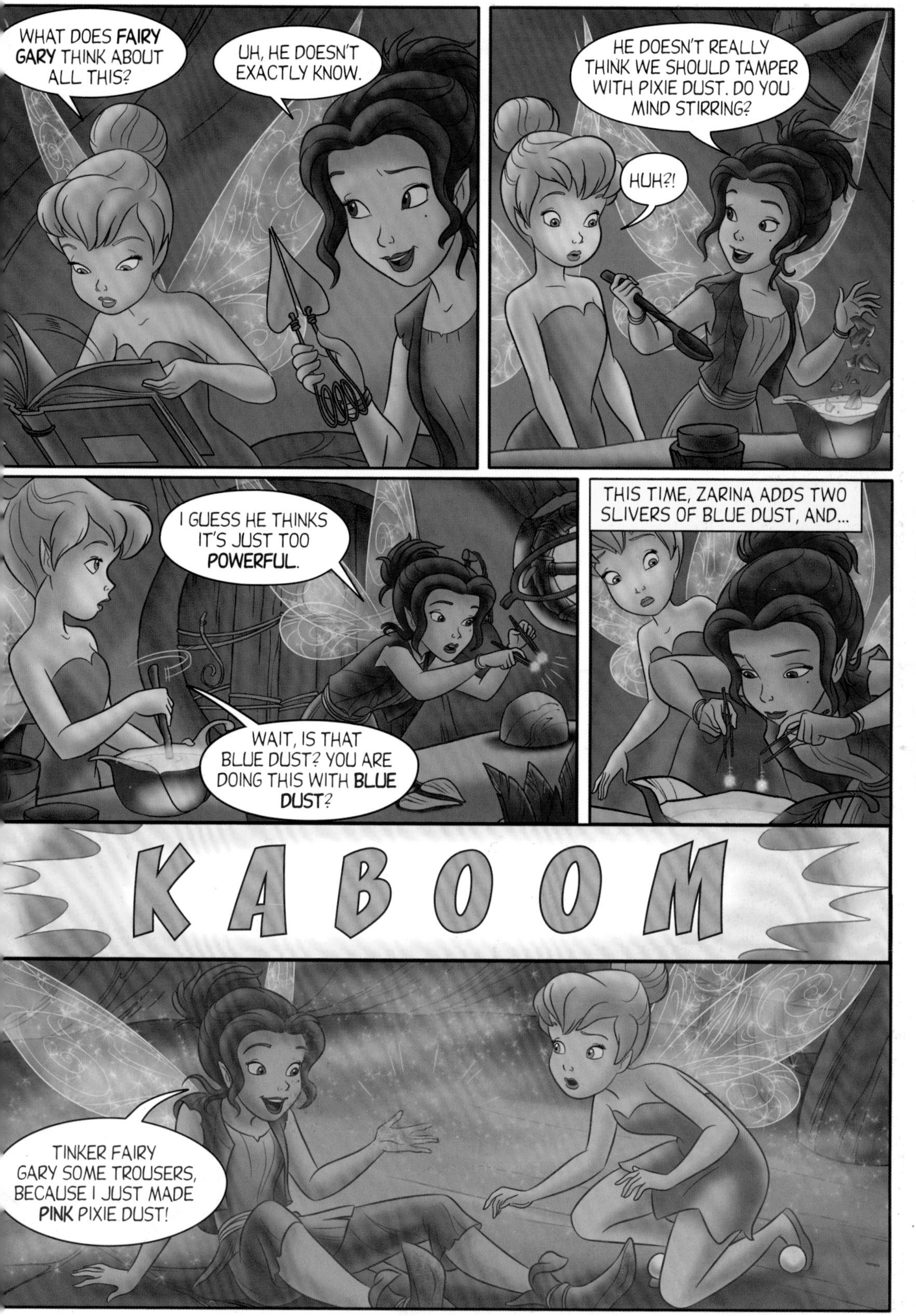
WHAT DOES **FAIRY GARY** THINK ABOUT ALL THIS?
UH, HE DOESN'T EXACTLY KNOW.
HE DOESN'T REALLY THINK WE SHOULD TAMPER WITH PIXIE DUST. DO YOU MIND STIRRING?
HUH?!
I GUESS HE THINKS IT'S JUST TOO **POWERFUL**.
WAIT, IS THAT BLUE DUST? YOU ARE DOING THIS WITH **BLUE DUST**?
THIS TIME, ZARINA ADDS TWO SLIVERS OF BLUE DUST, AND...
KABOOM
TINKER FAIRY GARY SOME TROUSERS, BECAUSE I JUST MADE **PINK** PIXIE DUST!

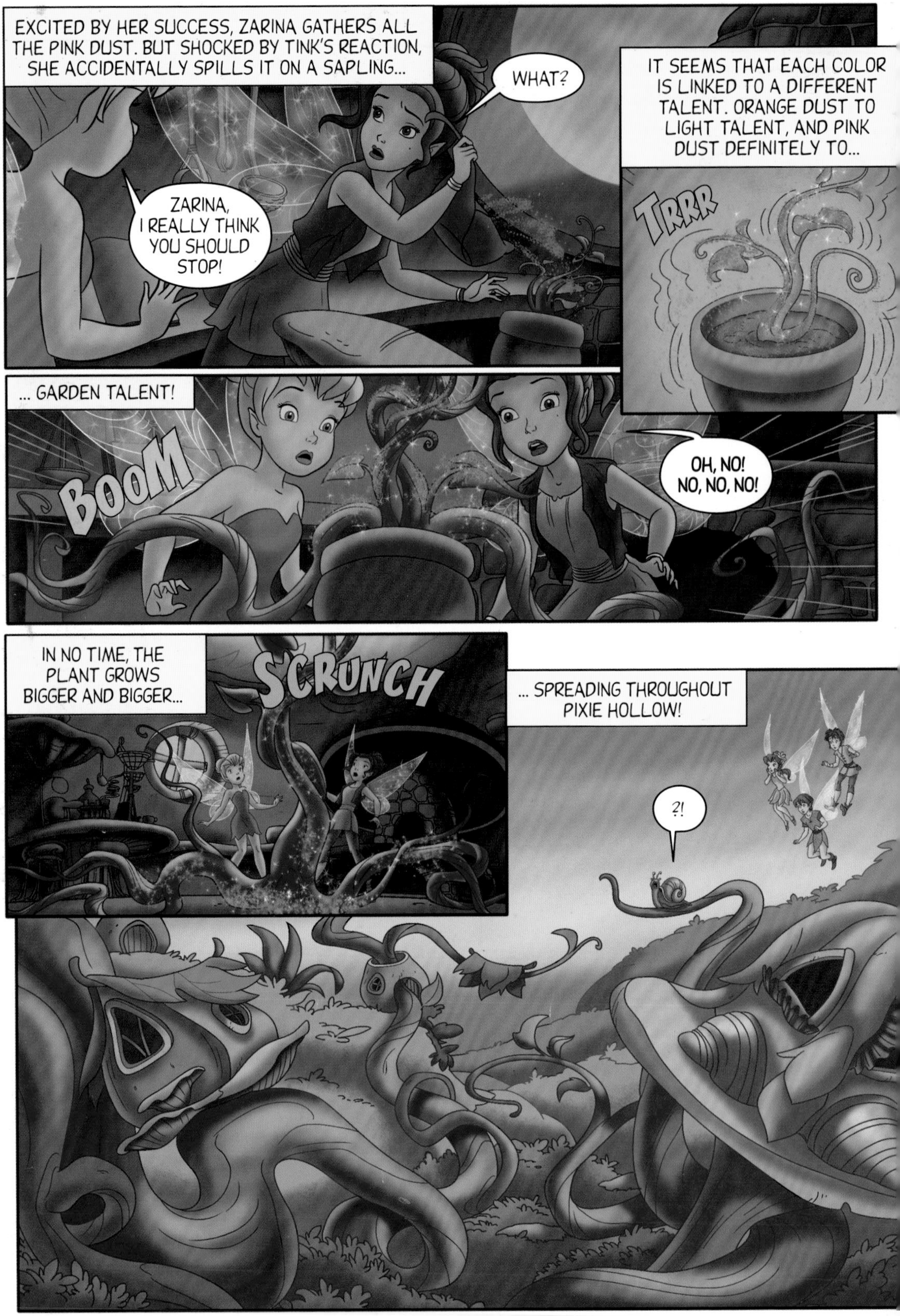
EXCITED BY HER SUCCESS, ZARINA GATHERS ALL THE PINK DUST. BUT SHOCKED BY TINK'S REACTION, SHE ACCIDENTALLY SPILLS IT ON A SAPLING...
WHAT?
ZARINA, I REALLY THINK YOU SHOULD STOP!
IT SEEMS THAT EACH COLOR IS LINKED TO A DIFFERENT TALENT. ORANGE DUST TO LIGHT TALENT, AND PINK DUST DEFINITELY TO...
TRRR
... GARDEN TALENT!
BOOM
OH, NO! NO, NO, NO!
IN NO TIME, THE PLANT GROWS BIGGER AND BIGGER...
SCRUNCH
... SPREADING THROUGHOUT PIXIE HOLLOW!
?!

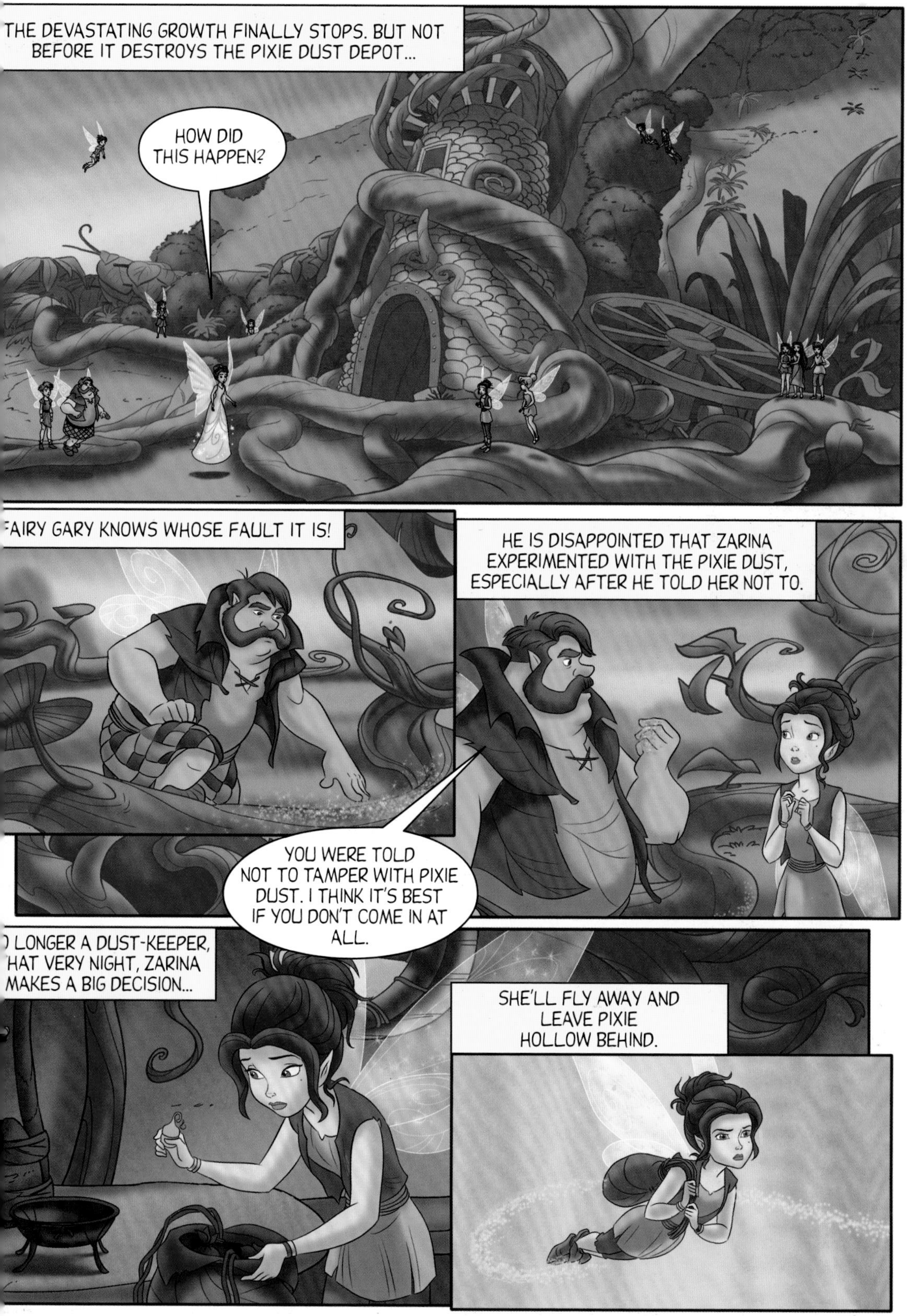
THE DEVASTATING GROWTH FINALLY STOPS. BUT NOT BEFORE IT DESTROYS THE PIXIE DUST DEPOT...
HOW DID THIS HAPPEN?
FAIRY GARY KNOWS WHOSE FAULT IT IS!
HE IS DISAPPOINTED THAT ZARINA EXPERIMENTED WITH THE PIXIE DUST, ESPECIALLY AFTER HE TOLD HER NOT TO.
YOU WERE TOLD NOT TO TAMPER WITH PIXIE DUST. I THINK IT'S BEST IF YOU DON'T COME IN AT ALL.
O LONGER A DUST-KEEPER, HAT VERY NIGHT, ZARINA MAKES A BIG DECISION...
SHE'LL FLY AWAY AND LEAVE PIXIE HOLLOW BEHIND.

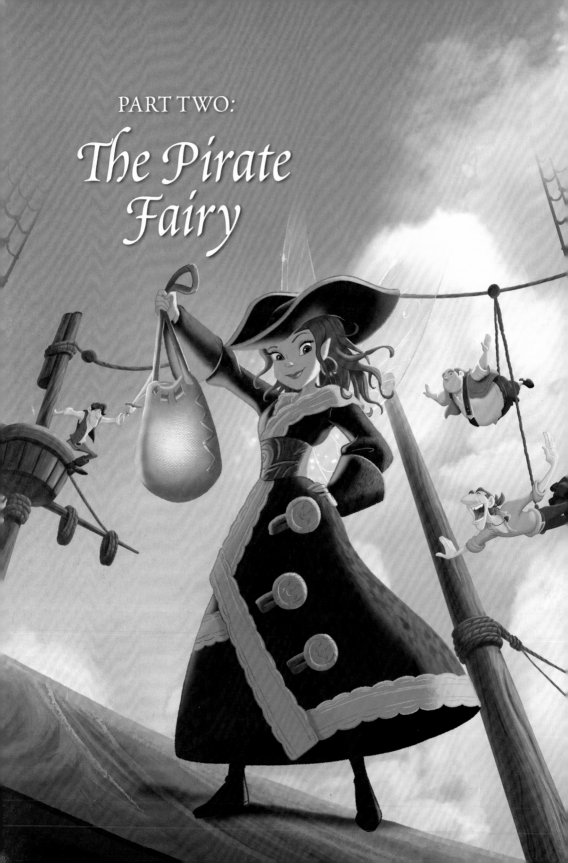

PART TWO:

# The Pirate Fairy

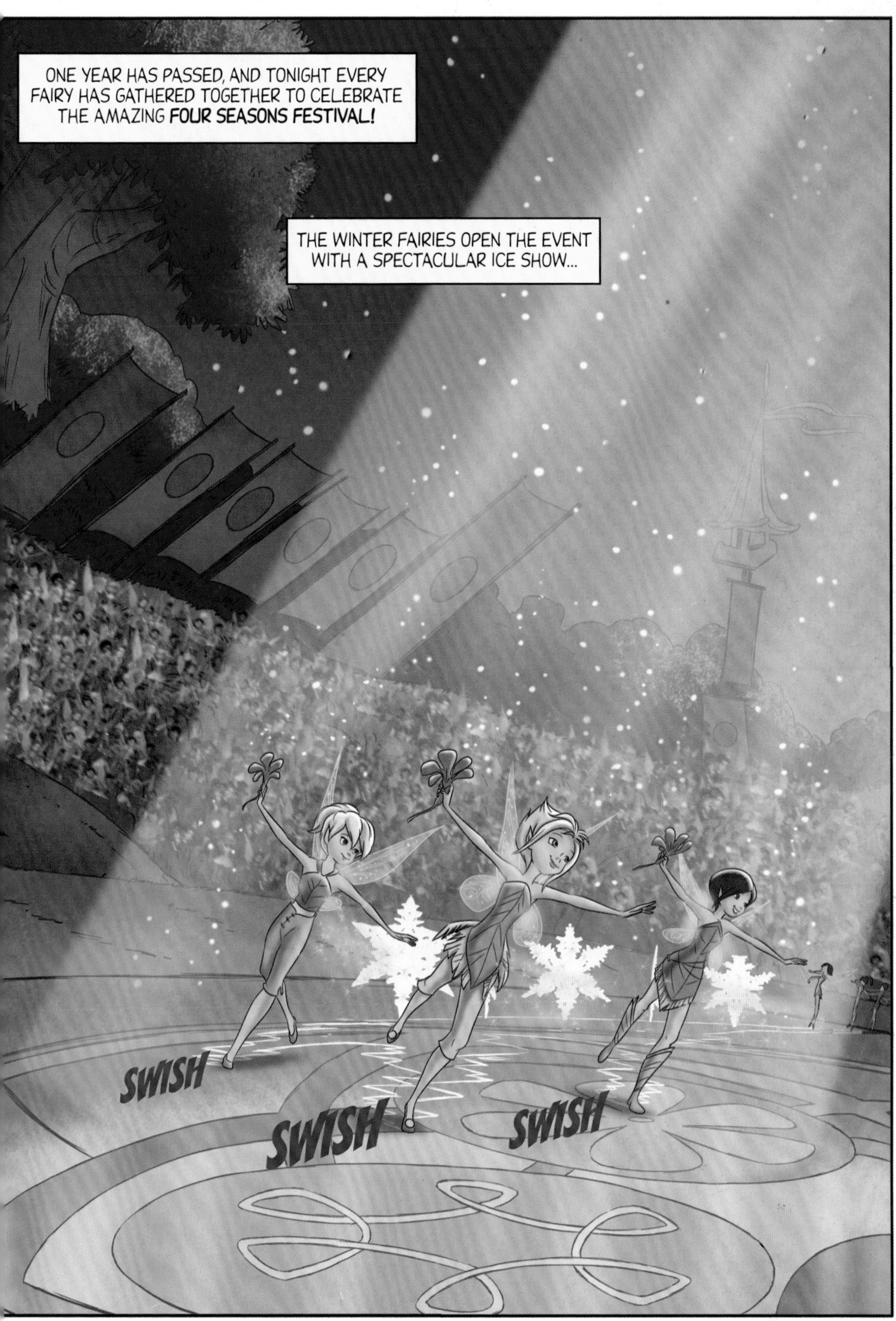
ONE YEAR HAS PASSED, AND TONIGHT EVERY FAIRY HAS GATHERED TOGETHER TO CELEBRATE THE AMAZING **FOUR SEASONS FESTIVAL!**
THE WINTER FAIRIES OPEN THE EVENT WITH A SPECTACULAR ICE SHOW...
SWISH
SWISH
SWISH

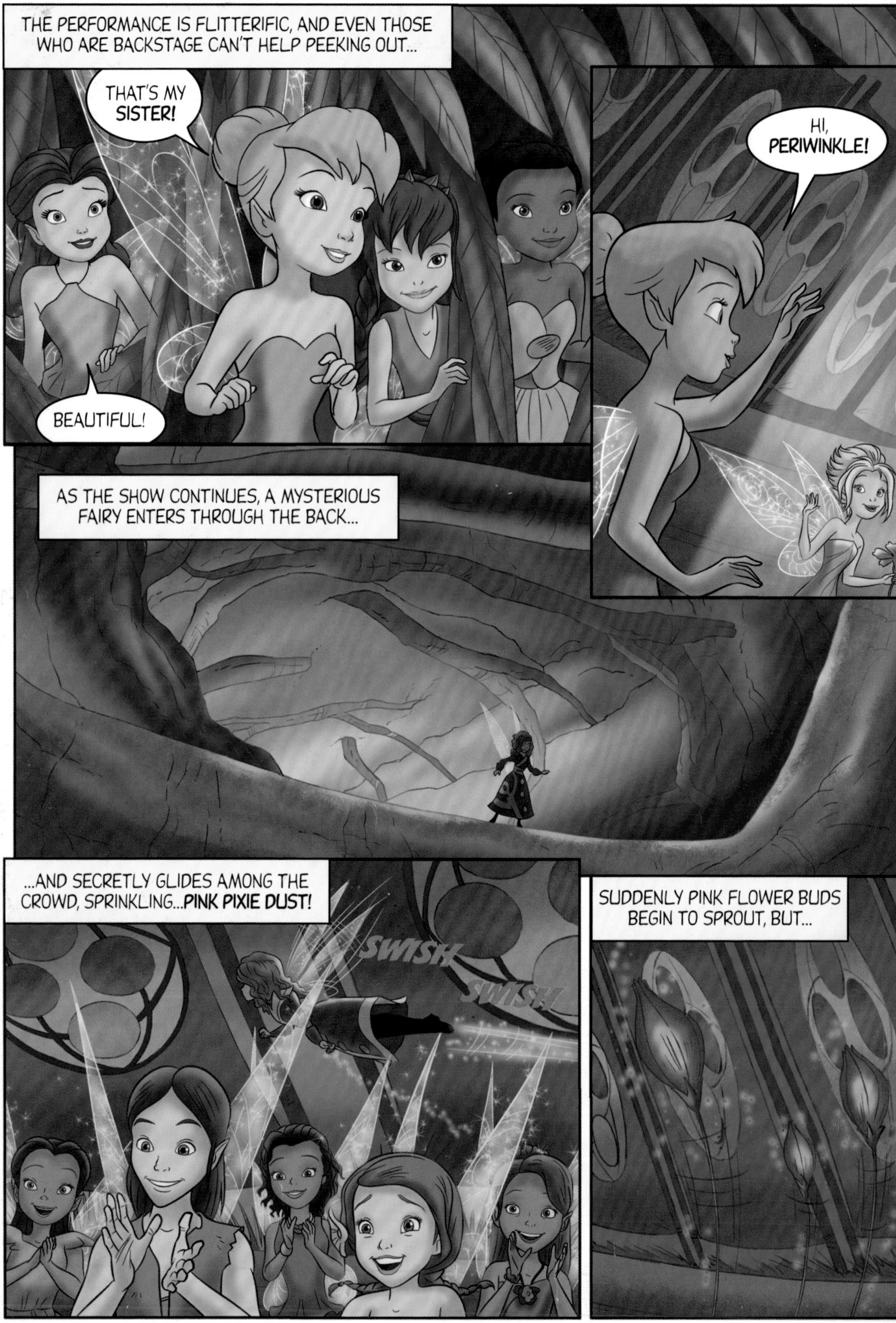
THE PERFORMANCE IS FLITTERIFIC, AND EVEN THOSE WHO ARE BACKSTAGE CAN'T HELP PEEKING OUT...
THAT'S MY SISTER!
BEAUTIFUL!
HI, PERIWINKLE!
AS THE SHOW CONTINUES, A MYSTERIOUS FAIRY ENTERS THROUGH THE BACK...
...AND SECRETLY GLIDES AMONG THE CROWD, SPRINKLING...PINK PIXIE DUST!
SWISH
SWISH
SUDDENLY PINK FLOWER BUDS BEGIN TO SPROUT, BUT...

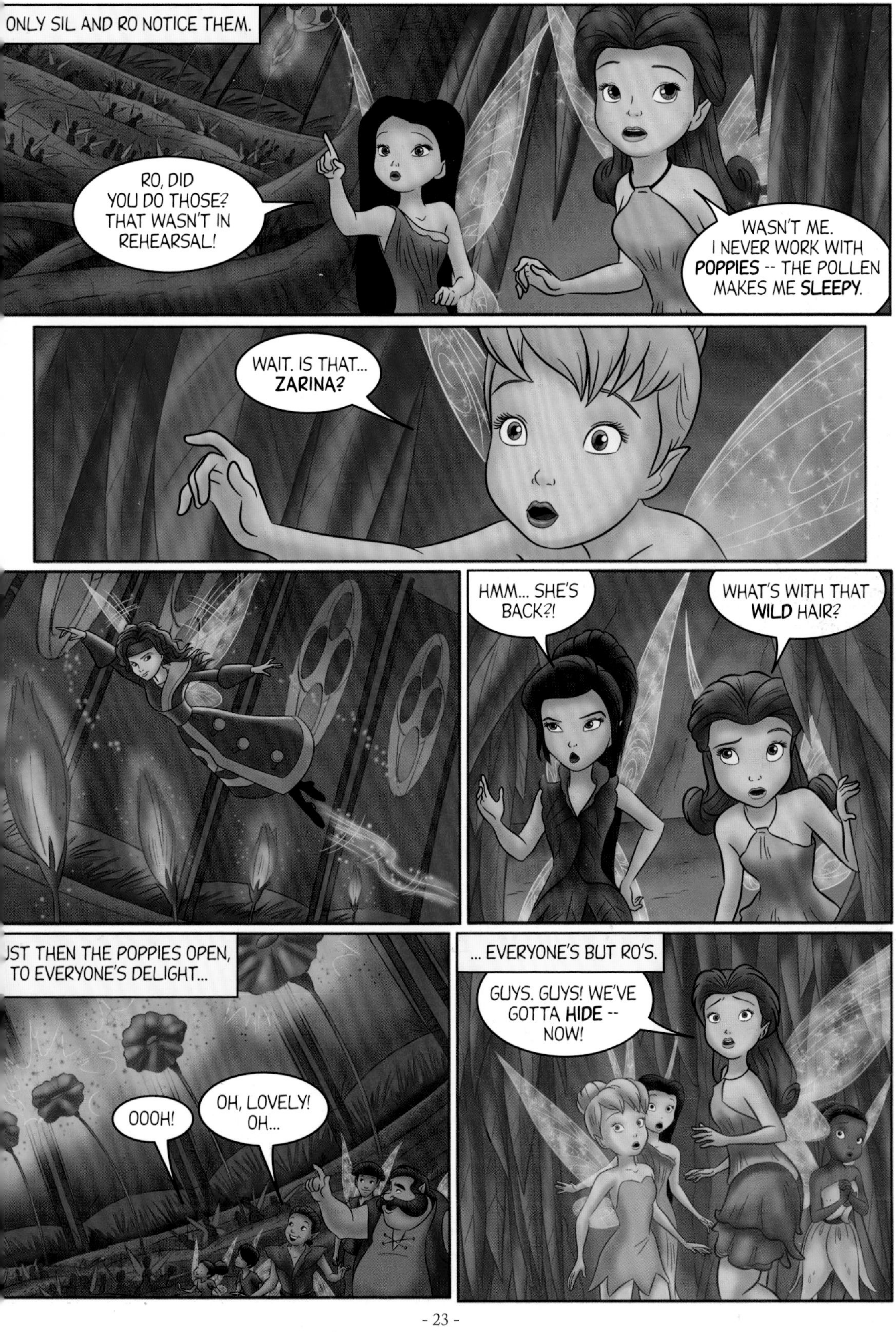

ONLY SIL AND RO NOTICE THEM.
RO, DID YOU DO THOSE? THAT WASN'T IN REHEARSAL!
WASN'T ME. I NEVER WORK WITH **POPPIES** -- THE POLLEN MAKES ME **SLEEPY**.
WAIT. IS THAT... **ZARINA?**
HMM... SHE'S BACK?!
WHAT'S WITH THAT **WILD** HAIR?
JST THEN THE POPPIES OPEN, TO EVERYONE'S DELIGHT...
OOOH!
OH, LOVELY! OH...
... EVERYONE'S BUT RO'S.
GUYS. GUYS! WE'VE GOTTA **HIDE** -- NOW!

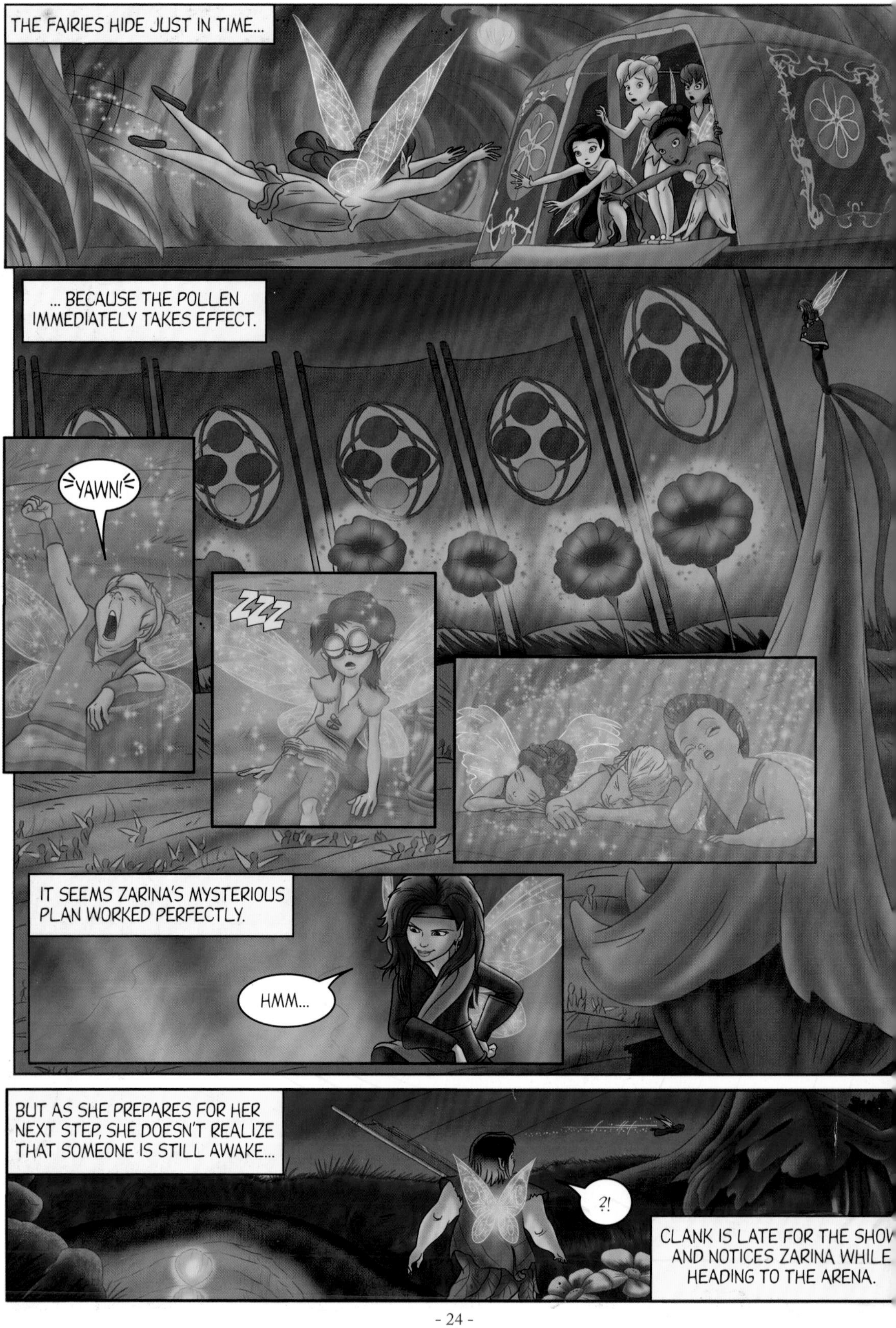
THE FAIRIES HIDE JUST IN TIME...
... BECAUSE THE POLLEN IMMEDIATELY TAKES EFFECT.
YAWN!
ZZZ
IT SEEMS ZARINA'S MYSTERIOUS PLAN WORKED PERFECTLY.
HMM...
BUT AS SHE PREPARES FOR HER NEXT STEP, SHE DOESN'T REALIZE THAT SOMEONE IS STILL AWAKE...
?!
CLANK IS LATE FOR THE SHOW AND NOTICES ZARINA WHILE HEADING TO THE ARENA.

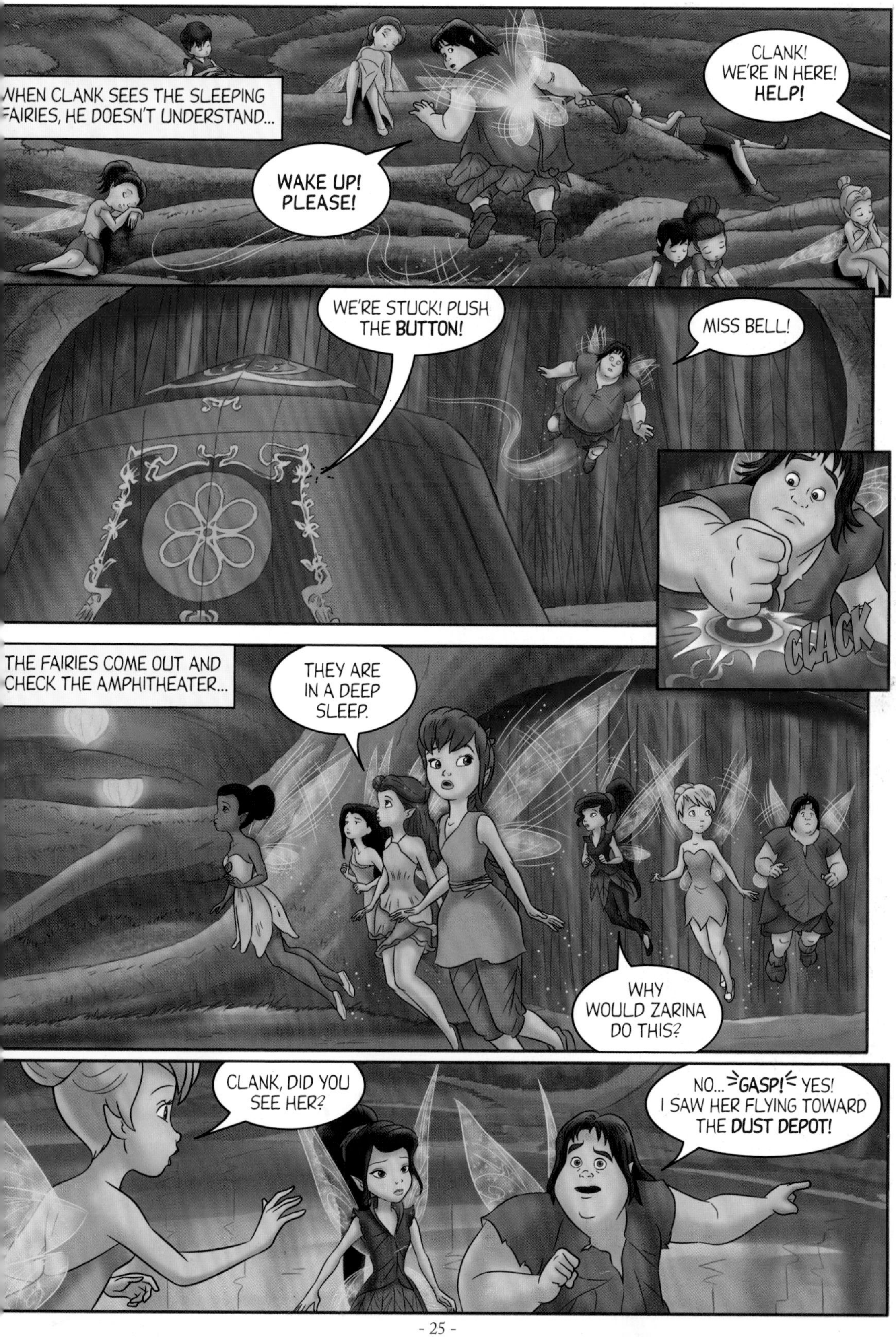
WHEN CLANK SEES THE SLEEPING FAIRIES, HE DOESN'T UNDERSTAND...
CLANK! WE'RE IN HERE! HELP!
WAKE UP! PLEASE!
WE'RE STUCK! PUSH THE BUTTON!
MISS BELL!
CLACK
THE FAIRIES COME OUT AND CHECK THE AMPHITHEATER...
THEY ARE IN A DEEP SLEEP.
WHY WOULD ZARINA DO THIS?
CLANK, DID YOU SEE HER?
NO... GASP! YES! I SAW HER FLYING TOWARD THE DUST DEPOT!

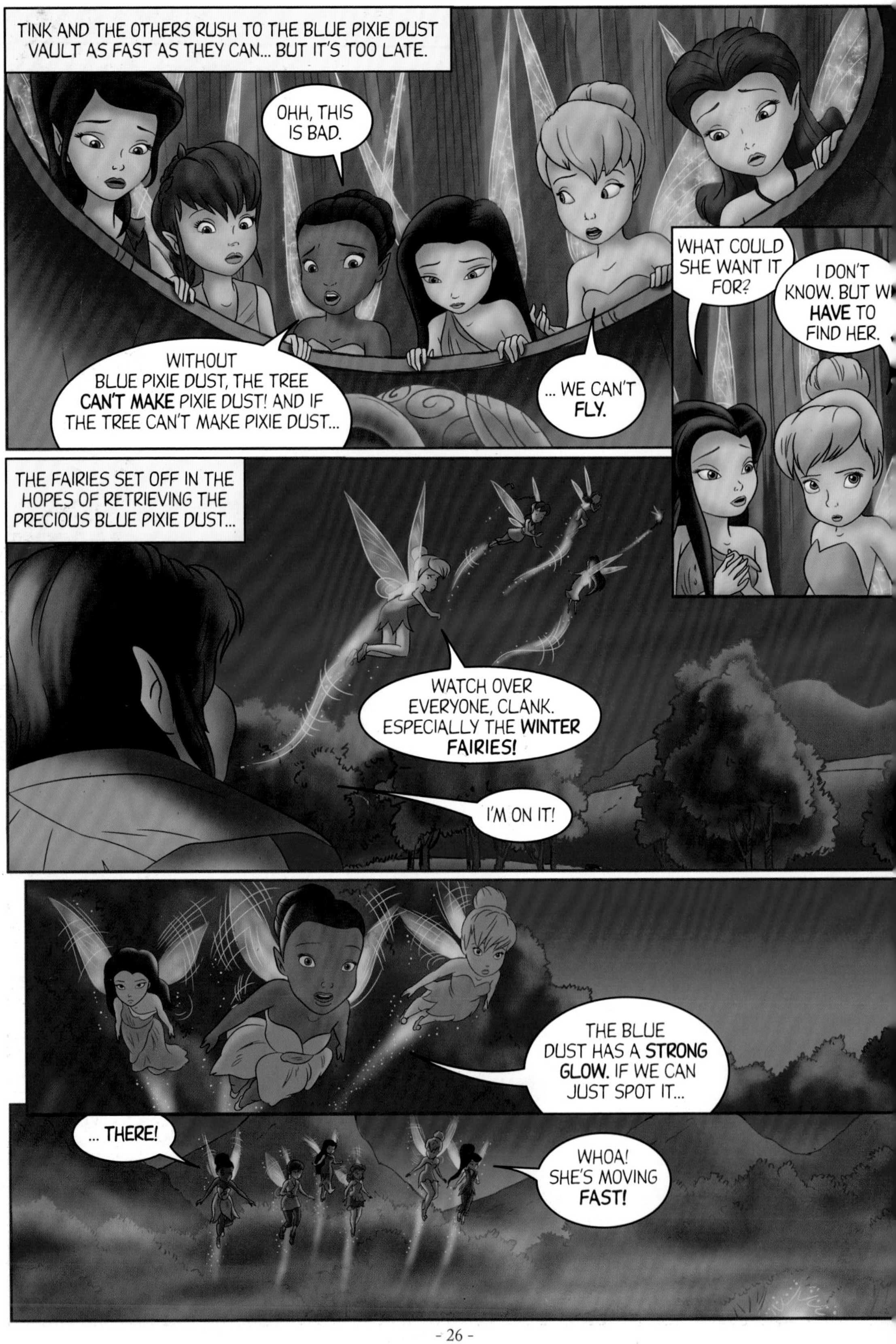

TINK AND THE OTHERS RUSH TO THE BLUE PIXIE DUST VAULT AS FAST AS THEY CAN... BUT IT'S TOO LATE.
OHH, THIS IS BAD.
WITHOUT BLUE PIXIE DUST, THE TREE CAN'T MAKE PIXIE DUST! AND IF THE TREE CAN'T MAKE PIXIE DUST...
... WE CAN'T FLY.
WHAT COULD SHE WANT IT FOR?
I DON'T KNOW. BUT W HAVE TO FIND HER.
THE FAIRIES SET OFF IN THE HOPES OF RETRIEVING THE PRECIOUS BLUE PIXIE DUST...
WATCH OVER EVERYONE, CLANK. ESPECIALLY THE WINTER FAIRIES!
I'M ON IT!
THE BLUE DUST HAS A STRONG GLOW. IF WE CAN JUST SPOT IT...
... THERE!
WHOA! SHE'S MOVING FAST!

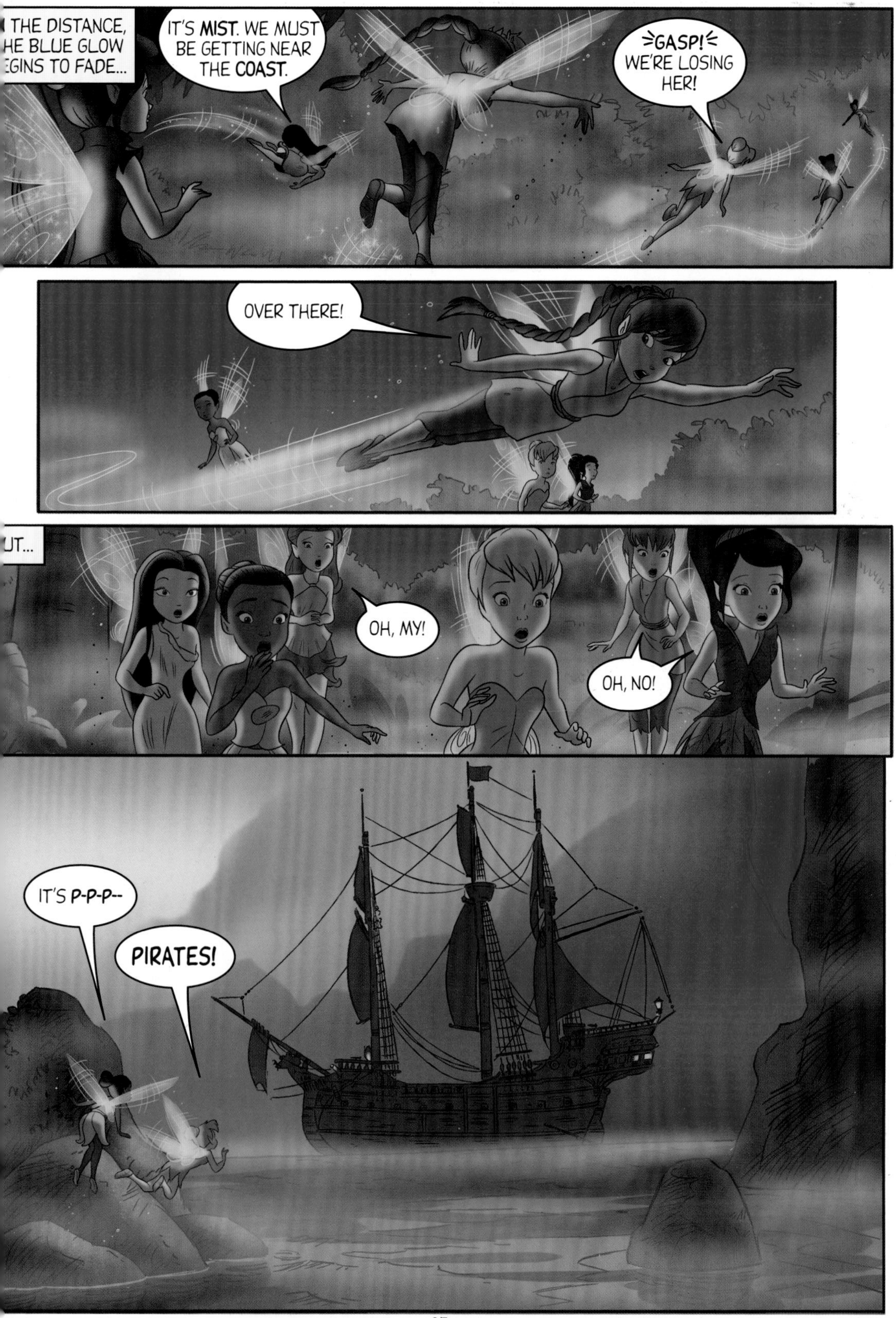

THE DISTANCE, HE BLUE GLOW EGINS TO FADE...
IT'S MIST. WE MUST BE GETTING NEAR THE COAST.
GASP! WE'RE LOSING HER!
OVER THERE!
UT...
OH, MY!
OH, NO!
IT'S P-P-P--
PIRATES!

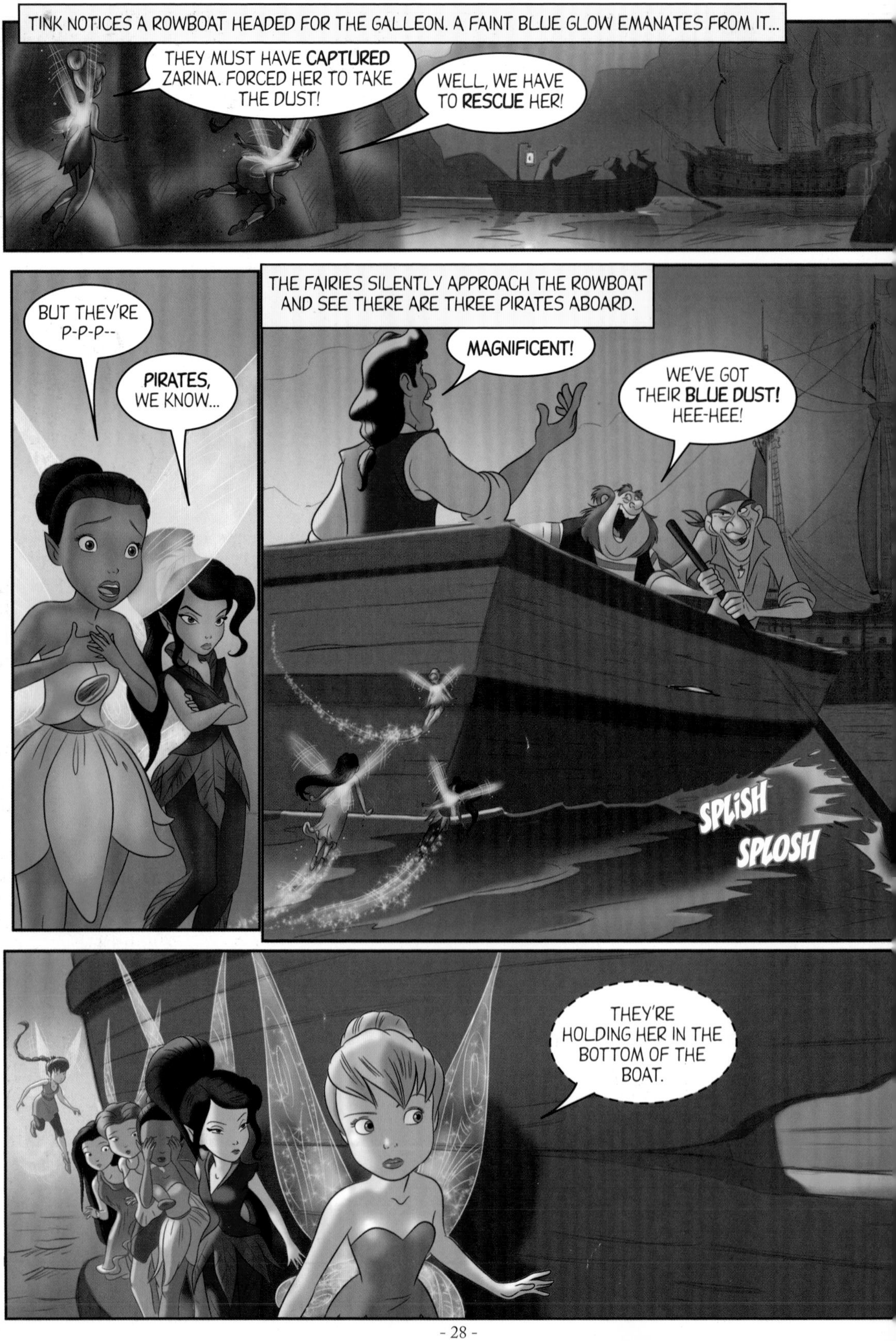

TINK NOTICES A ROWBOAT HEADED FOR THE GALLEON. A FAINT BLUE GLOW EMANATES FROM IT...
THEY MUST HAVE **CAPTURED** ZARINA. FORCED HER TO TAKE THE DUST!
WELL, WE HAVE TO **RESCUE** HER!
BUT THEY'RE P-P-P--
**PIRATES,** WE KNOW...
THE FAIRIES SILENTLY APPROACH THE ROWBOAT AND SEE THERE ARE THREE PIRATES ABOARD.
**MAGNIFICENT!**
WE'VE GOT THEIR **BLUE DUST!** HEE-HEE!
SPLISH
SPLOSH
THEY'RE HOLDING HER IN THE BOTTOM OF THE BOAT.

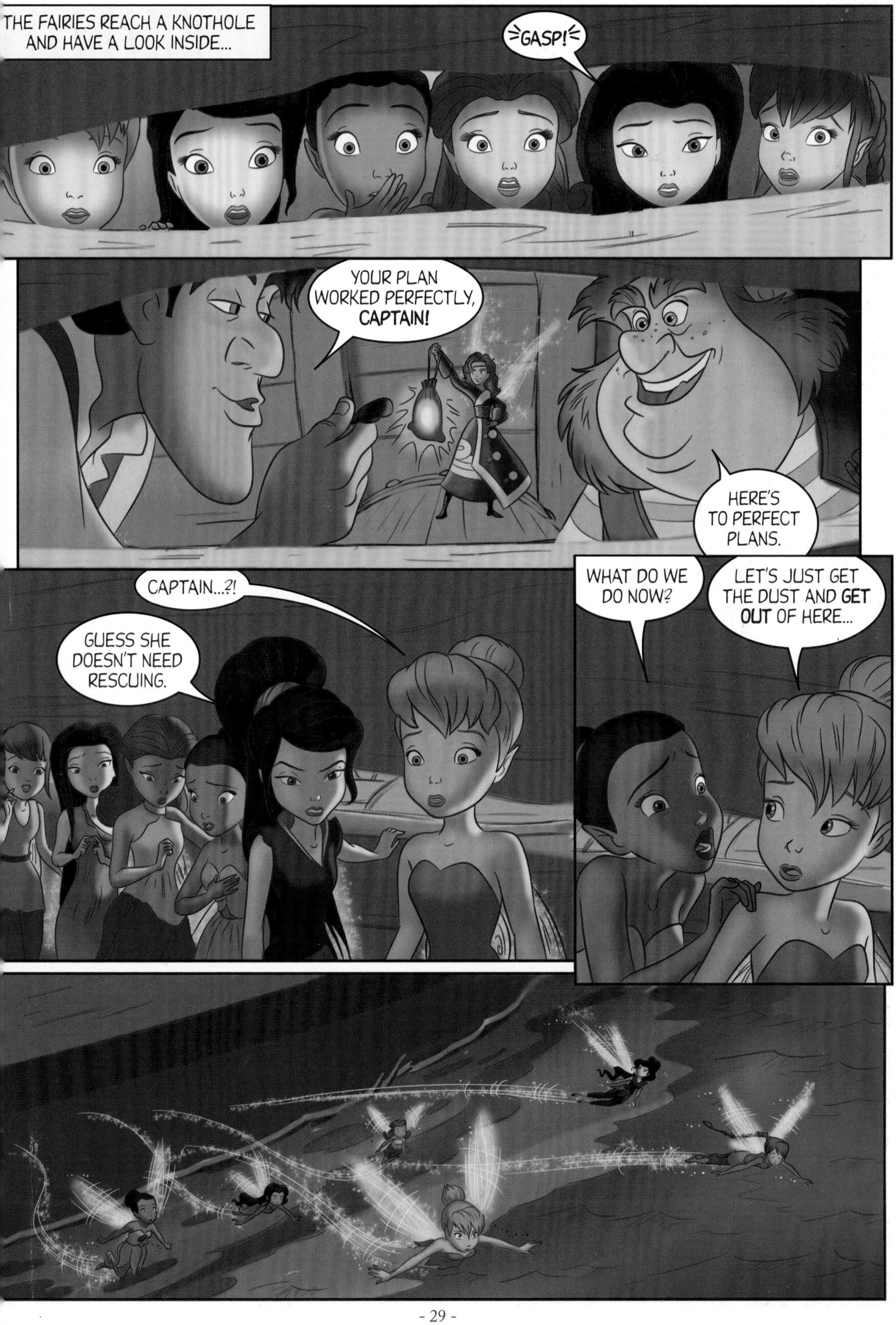
THE FAIRIES REACH A KNOTHOLE AND HAVE A LOOK INSIDE...
GASP!
YOUR PLAN WORKED PERFECTLY, CAPTAIN!
HERE'S TO PERFECT PLANS.
CAPTAIN...?!
GUESS SHE DOESN'T NEED RESCUING.
WHAT DO WE DO NOW?
LET'S JUST GET THE DUST AND GET OUT OF HERE...

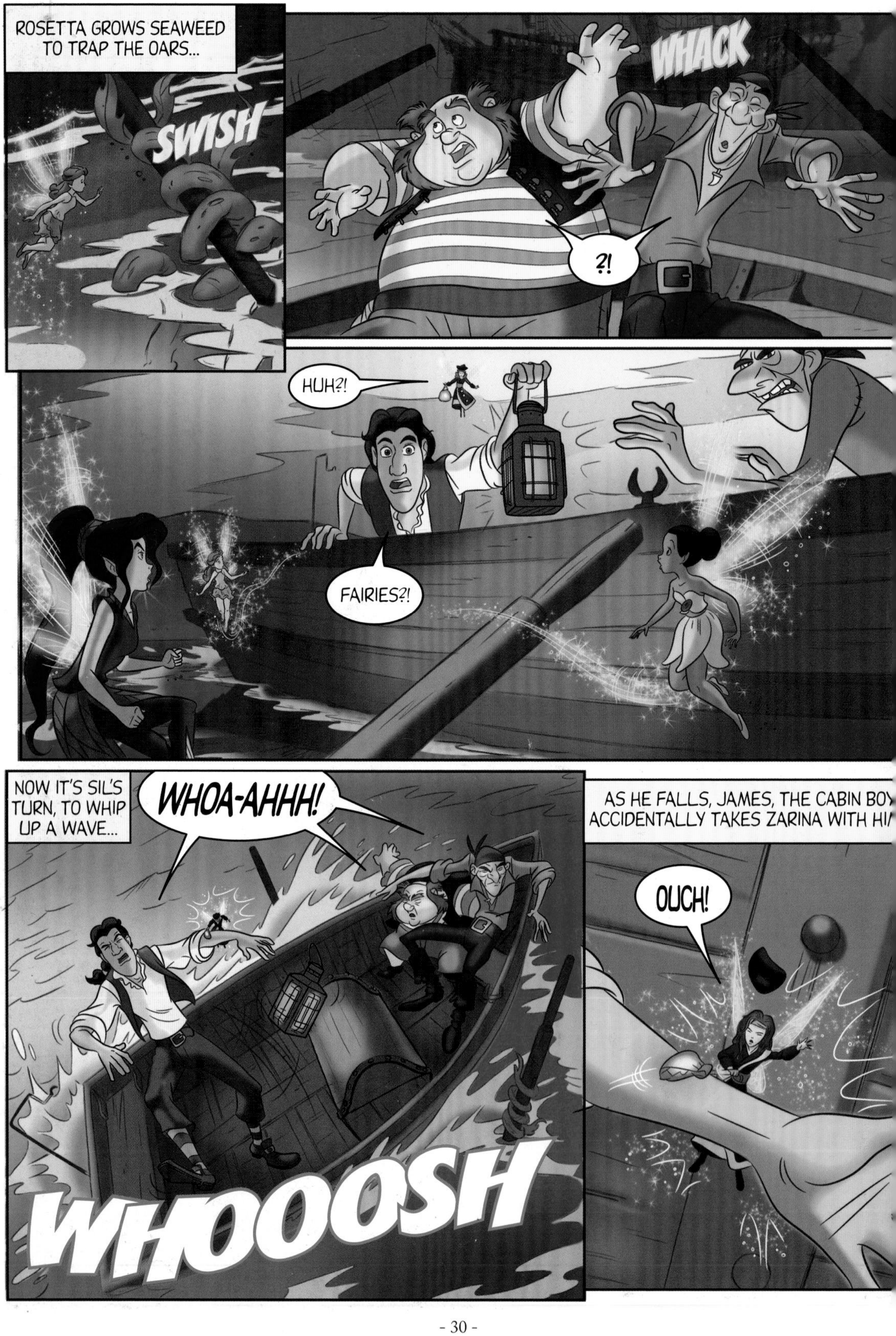
ROSETTA GROWS SEAWEED TO TRAP THE OARS...
SWISH
WHACK
?!
HUH?!
FAIRIES?!
NOW IT'S SIL'S TURN, TO WHIP UP A WAVE...
WHOA-AHHH!
WHOOOSH
AS HE FALLS, JAMES, THE CABIN BOY ACCIDENTALLY TAKES ZARINA WITH HI
OUCH!

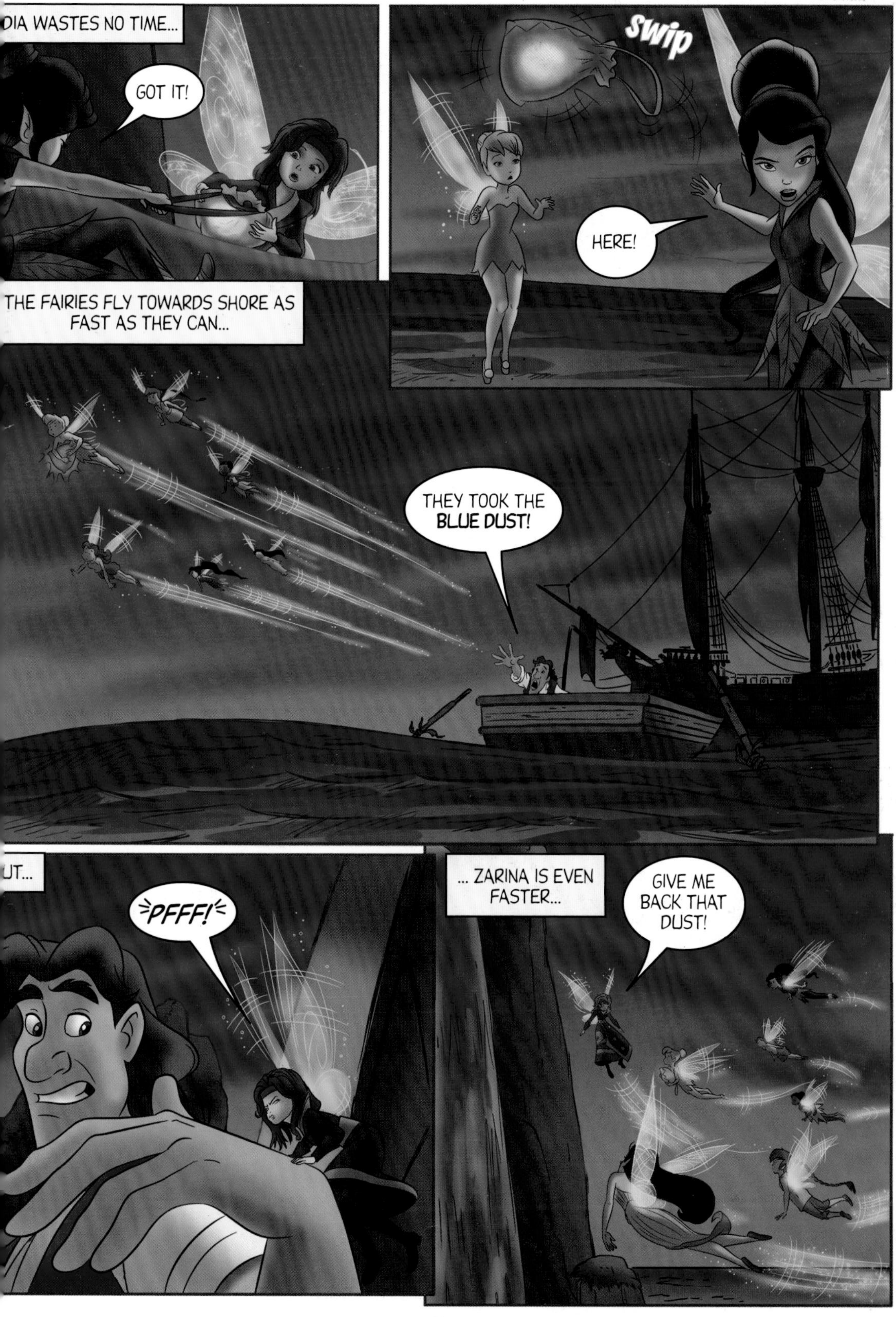
DIA WASTES NO TIME...
GOT IT!
SWIP
HERE!
THE FAIRIES FLY TOWARDS SHORE AS FAST AS THEY CAN...
THEY TOOK THE **BLUE DUST!**
UT...
PFFF!
... ZARINA IS EVEN FASTER...
GIVE ME BACK THAT DUST!

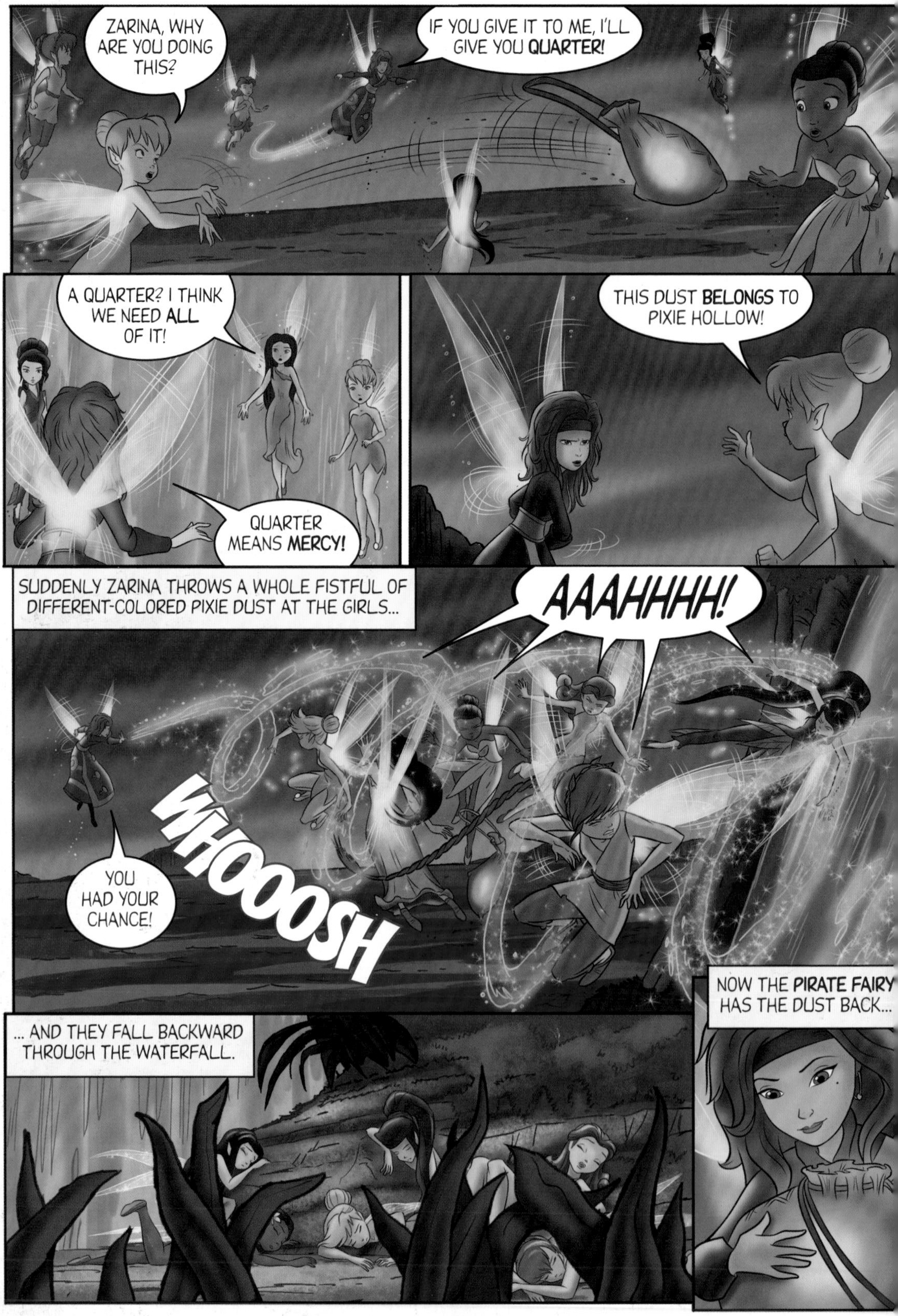
ZARINA, WHY ARE YOU DOING THIS?
IF YOU GIVE IT TO ME, I'LL GIVE YOU QUARTER!
A QUARTER? I THINK WE NEED ALL OF IT!
QUARTER MEANS MERCY!
THIS DUST BELONGS TO PIXIE HOLLOW!
SUDDENLY ZARINA THROWS A WHOLE FISTFUL OF DIFFERENT-COLORED PIXIE DUST AT THE GIRLS...
AAAHHHH!
WHOOOOSH
YOU HAD YOUR CHANCE!
... AND THEY FALL BACKWARD THROUGH THE WATERFALL.
NOW THE PIRATE FAIRY HAS THE DUST BACK...

# PART THREE:
# *Prisoners*

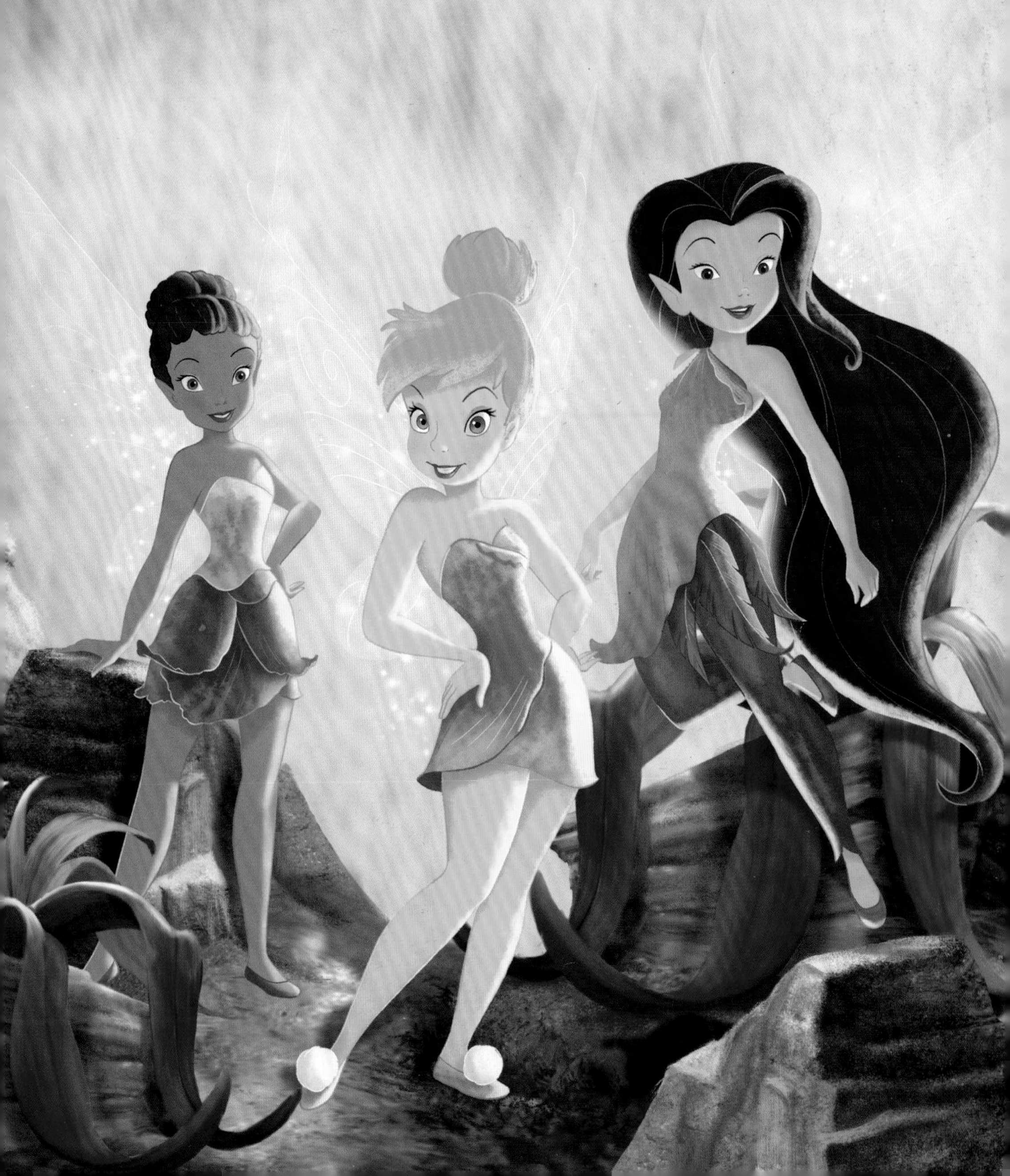

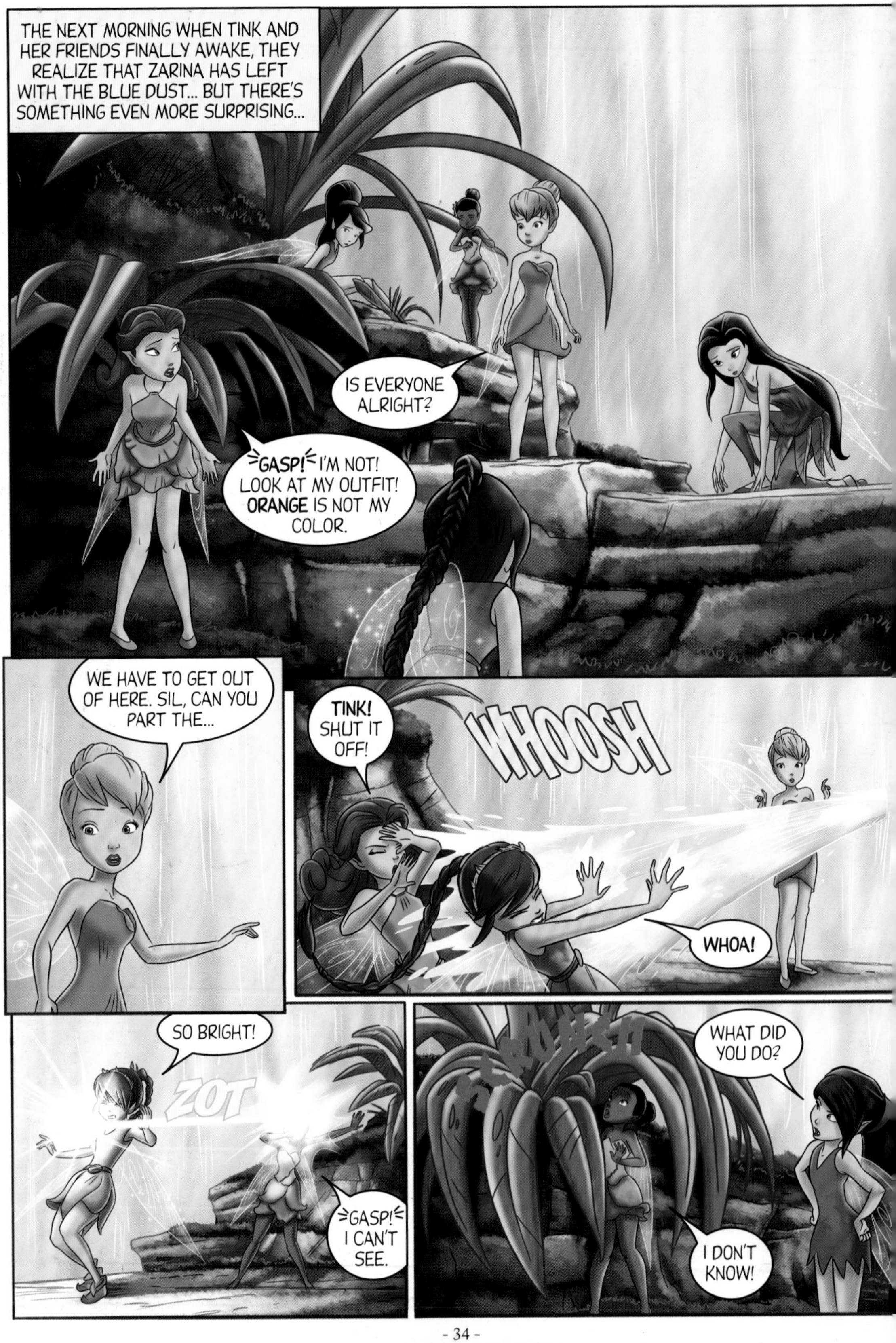
THE NEXT MORNING WHEN TINK AND HER FRIENDS FINALLY AWAKE, THEY REALIZE THAT ZARINA HAS LEFT WITH THE BLUE DUST... BUT THERE'S SOMETHING EVEN MORE SURPRISING...
IS EVERYONE ALRIGHT?
GASP! I'M NOT! LOOK AT MY OUTFIT! ORANGE IS NOT MY COLOR.
WE HAVE TO GET OUT OF HERE. SIL, CAN YOU PART THE...
TINK! SHUT IT OFF!
WHOOSH
WHOA!
SO BRIGHT!
ZOT
GASP! I CAN'T SEE.
WHAT DID YOU DO?
I DON'T KNOW!

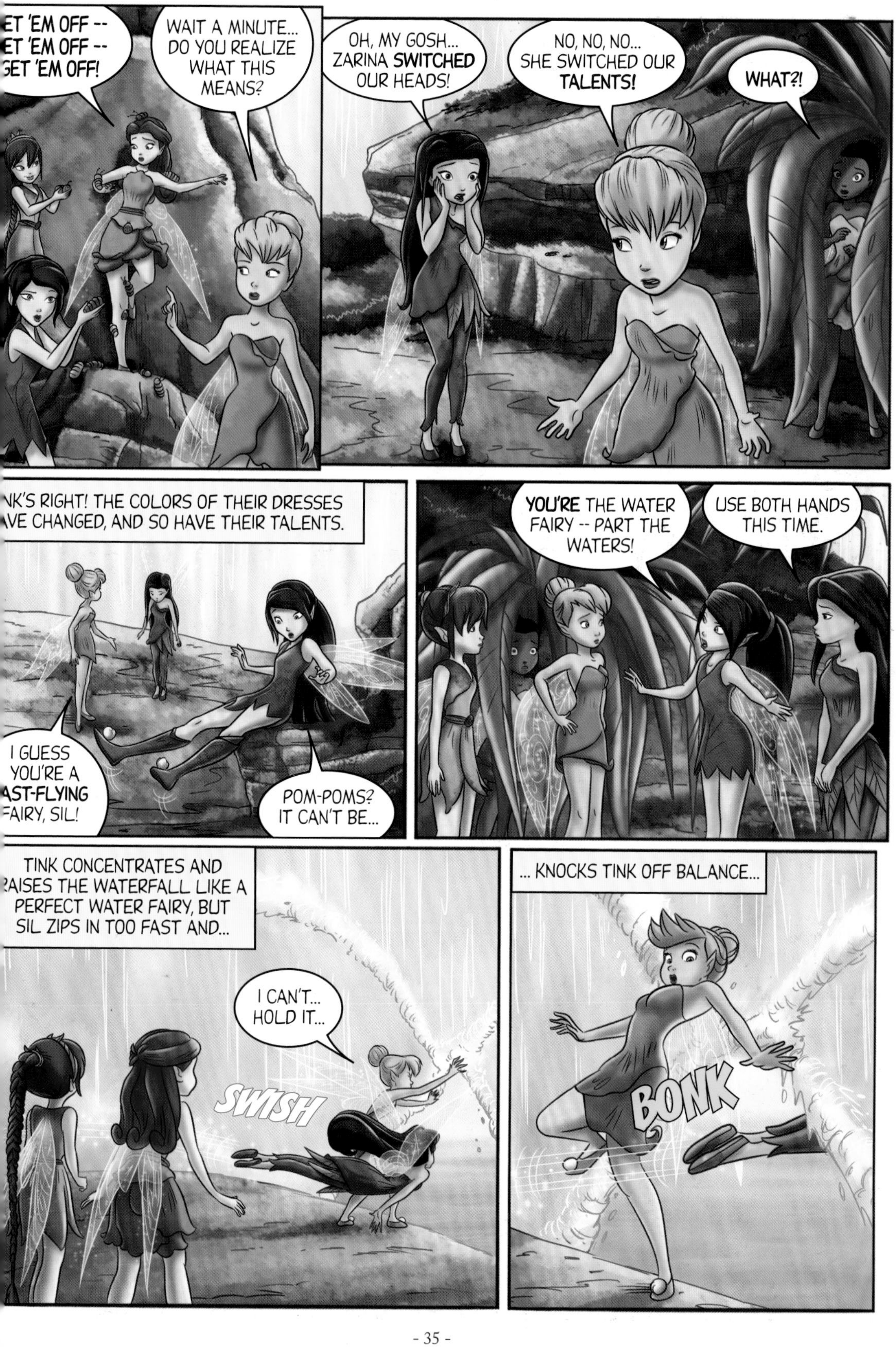
ET 'EM OFF --
ET 'EM OFF --
GET 'EM OFF!
WAIT A MINUTE... DO YOU REALIZE WHAT THIS MEANS?
OH, MY GOSH... ZARINA **SWITCHED** OUR HEADS!
NO, NO, NO... SHE SWITCHED OUR **TALENTS!**
**WHAT?!**
NK'S RIGHT! THE COLORS OF THEIR DRESSES
VE CHANGED, AND SO HAVE THEIR TALENTS.
I GUESS YOU'RE A **AST-FLYING** AIRY, SIL!
POM-POMS? IT CAN'T BE...
**YOU'RE** THE WATER FAIRY -- PART THE WATERS!
USE BOTH HANDS THIS TIME.
TINK CONCENTRATES AND AISES THE WATERFALL LIKE A PERFECT WATER FAIRY, BUT SIL ZIPS IN TOO FAST AND...
I CAN'T... HOLD IT...
SWISH
... KNOCKS TINK OFF BALANCE...
BONK

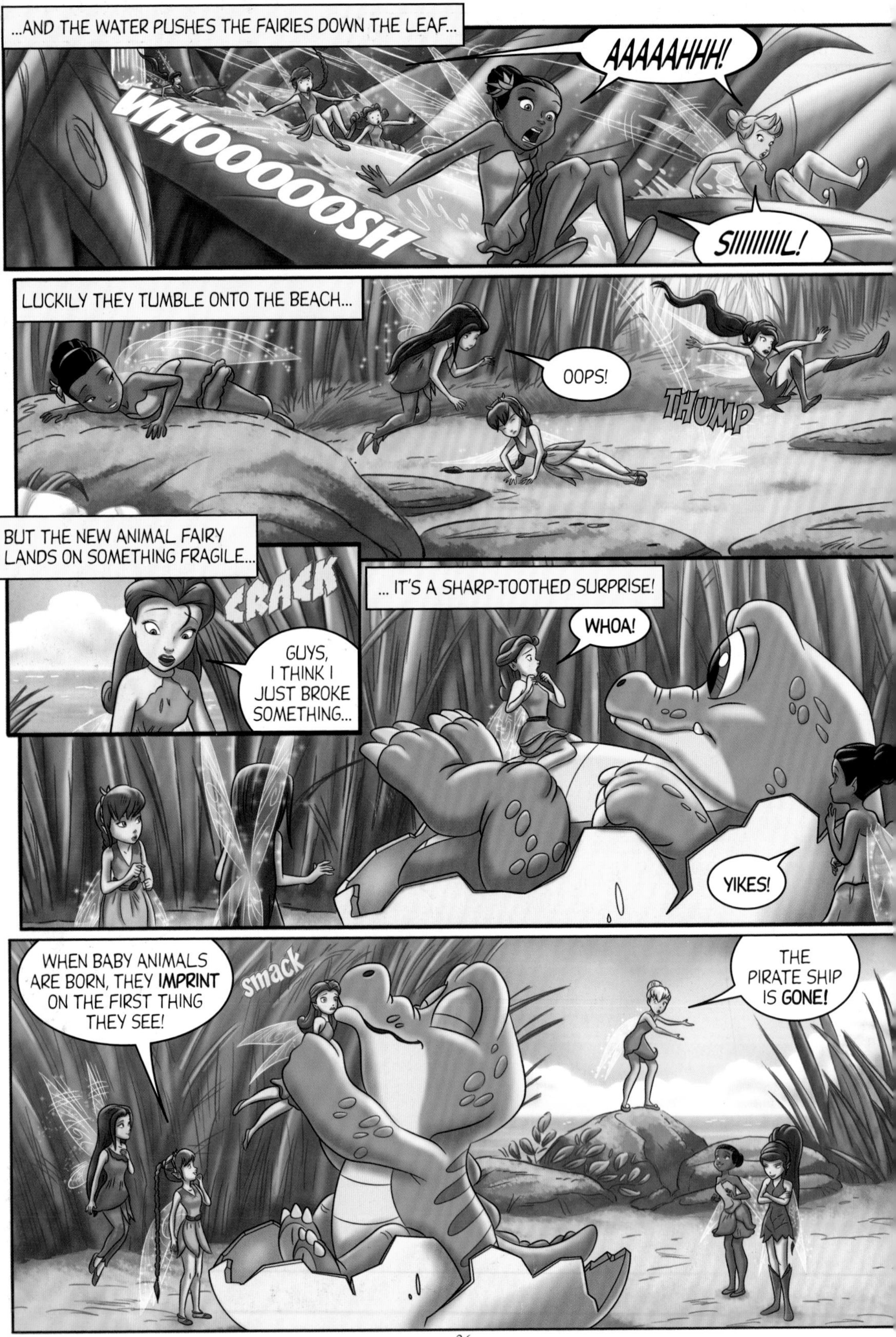
...AND THE WATER PUSHES THE FAIRIES DOWN THE LEAF...
WHOOOOOOSH
AAAAAHHH!
SIIIIIIIIL!
LUCKILY THEY TUMBLE ONTO THE BEACH...
OOPS!
THUMP
BUT THE NEW ANIMAL FAIRY LANDS ON SOMETHING FRAGILE...
CRACK
GUYS, I THINK I JUST BROKE SOMETHING...
... IT'S A SHARP-TOOTHED SURPRISE!
WHOA!
YIKES!
WHEN BABY ANIMALS ARE BORN, THEY **IMPRINT** ON THE FIRST THING THEY SEE!
smack
THE PIRATE SHIP IS **GONE!**

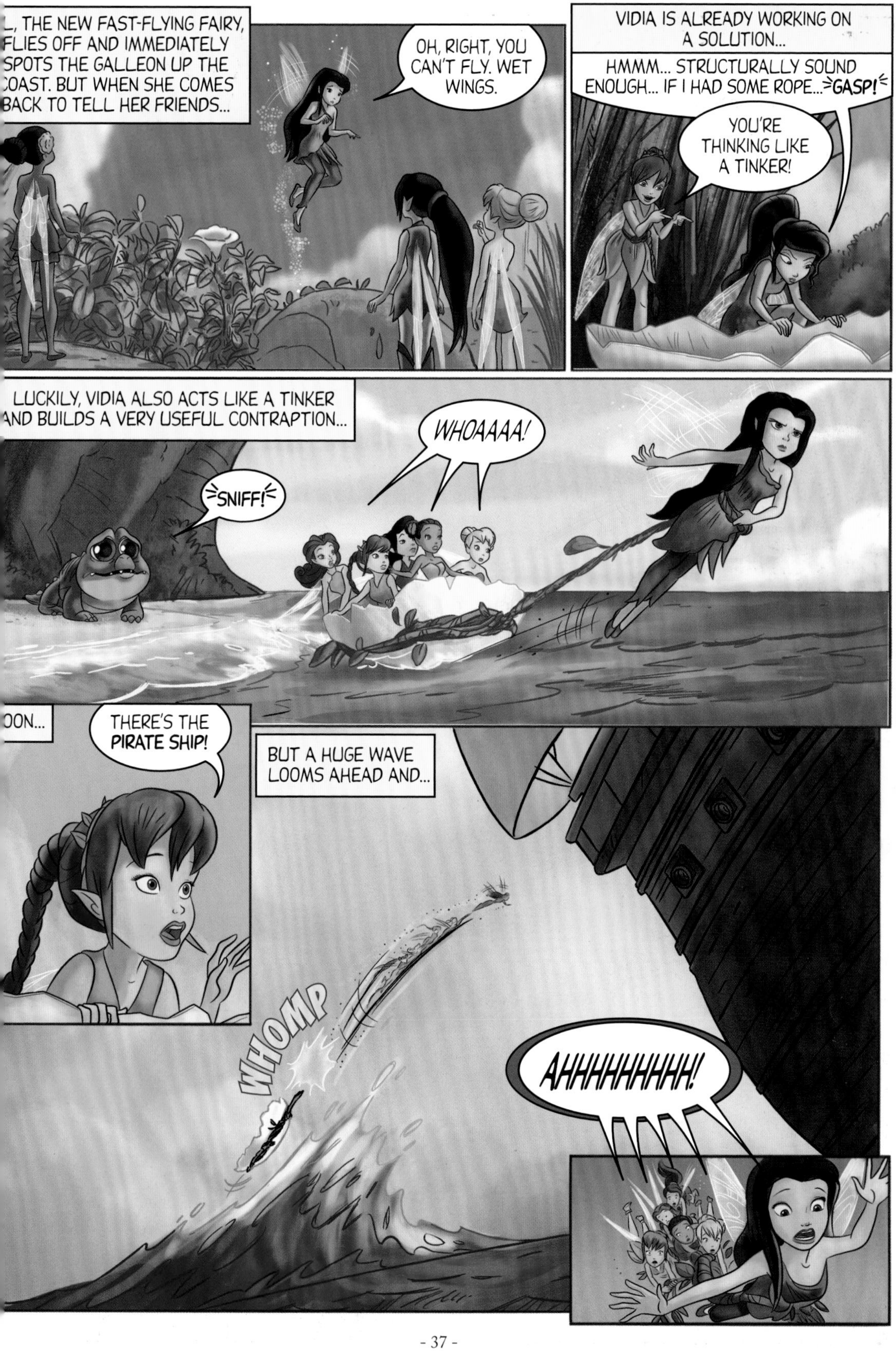

L, THE NEW FAST-FLYING FAIRY, FLIES OFF AND IMMEDIATELY SPOTS THE GALLEON UP THE COAST. BUT WHEN SHE COMES BACK TO TELL HER FRIENDS...
OH, RIGHT, YOU CAN'T FLY. WET WINGS.
VIDIA IS ALREADY WORKING ON A SOLUTION...
HMMM... STRUCTURALLY SOUND ENOUGH... IF I HAD SOME ROPE... GASP!
YOU'RE THINKING LIKE A TINKER!
LUCKILY, VIDIA ALSO ACTS LIKE A TINKER AND BUILDS A VERY USEFUL CONTRAPTION...
WHOAAAA!
SNIFF!
OON...
THERE'S THE PIRATE SHIP!
BUT A HUGE WAVE LOOMS AHEAD AND...
WHOMP
AHHHHHHHHH!

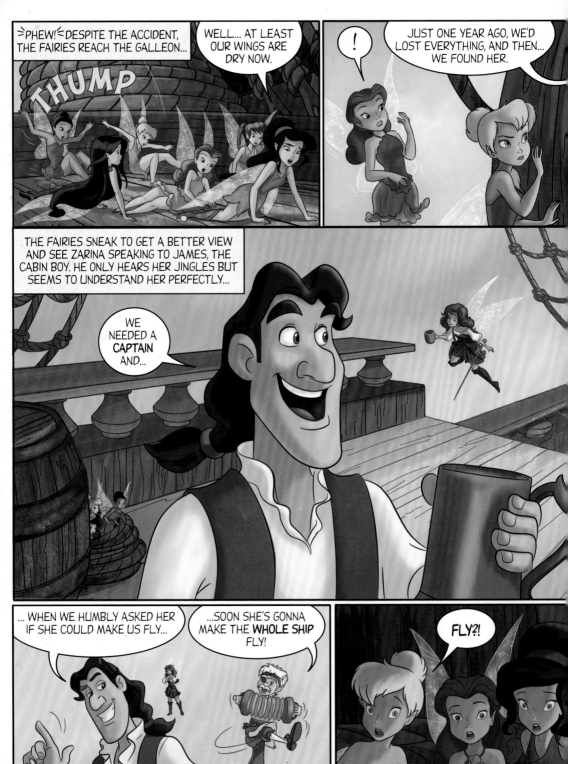

≥PHEW!≤ DESPITE THE ACCIDENT, THE FAIRIES REACH THE GALLEON...

WELL... AT LEAST OUR WINGS ARE DRY NOW.

THUMP

!

JUST ONE YEAR AGO, WE'D LOST EVERYTHING, AND THEN... WE FOUND HER.

THE FAIRIES SNEAK TO GET A BETTER VIEW AND SEE ZARINA SPEAKING TO JAMES, THE CABIN BOY. HE ONLY HEARS HER JINGLES BUT SEEMS TO UNDERSTAND HER PERFECTLY...

WE NEEDED A CAPTAIN AND...

... WHEN WE HUMBLY ASKED HER IF SHE COULD MAKE US FLY...

...SOON SHE'S GONNA MAKE THE WHOLE SHIP FLY!

FLY?!

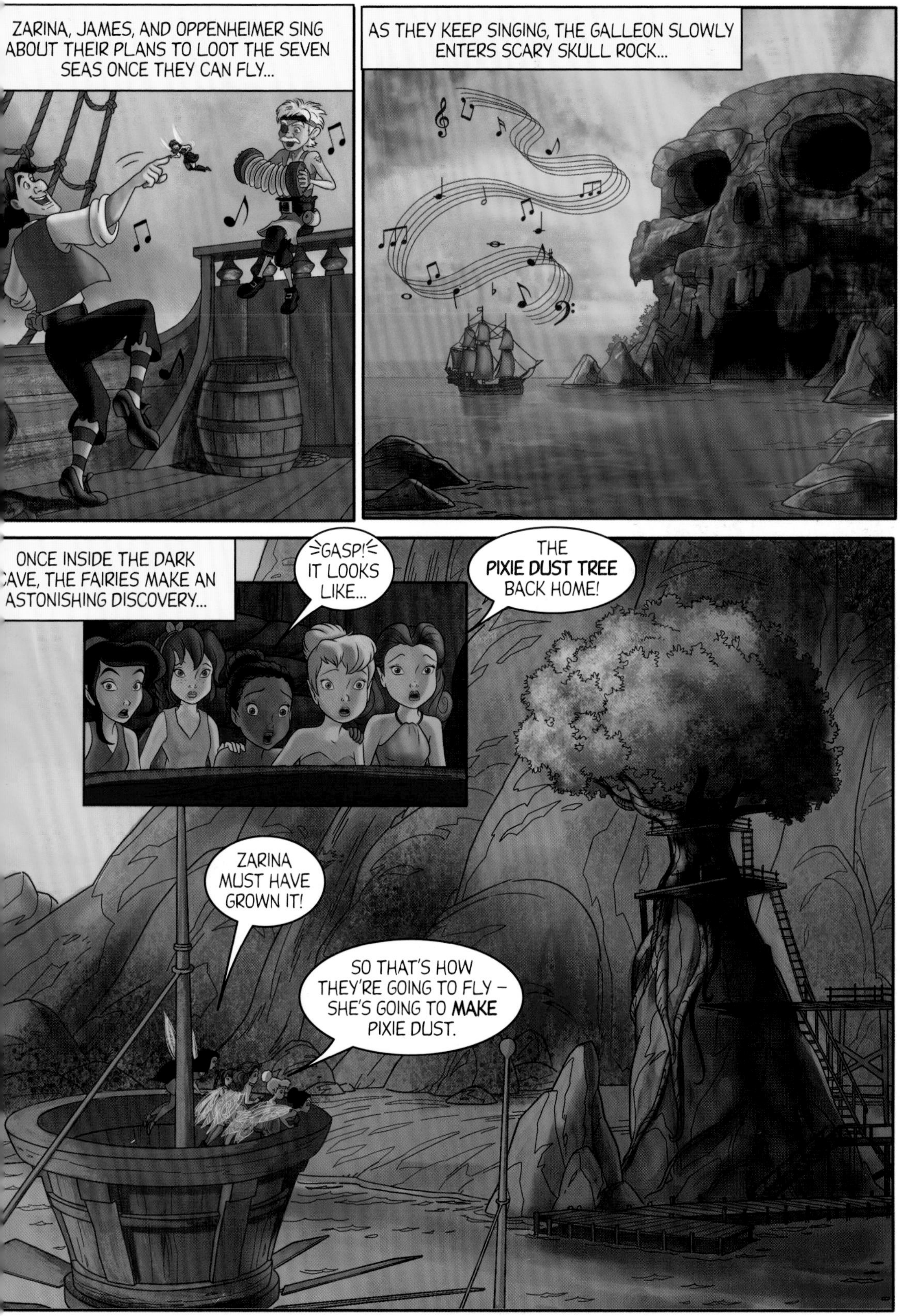

ZARINA, JAMES, AND OPPENHEIMER SING ABOUT THEIR PLANS TO LOOT THE SEVEN SEAS ONCE THEY CAN FLY...
AS THEY KEEP SINGING, THE GALLEON SLOWLY ENTERS SCARY SKULL ROCK...
ONCE INSIDE THE DARK CAVE, THE FAIRIES MAKE AN ASTONISHING DISCOVERY...
GASP! IT LOOKS LIKE...
THE PIXIE DUST TREE BACK HOME!
ZARINA MUST HAVE GROWN IT!
SO THAT'S HOW THEY'RE GOING TO FLY – SHE'S GOING TO MAKE PIXIE DUST.

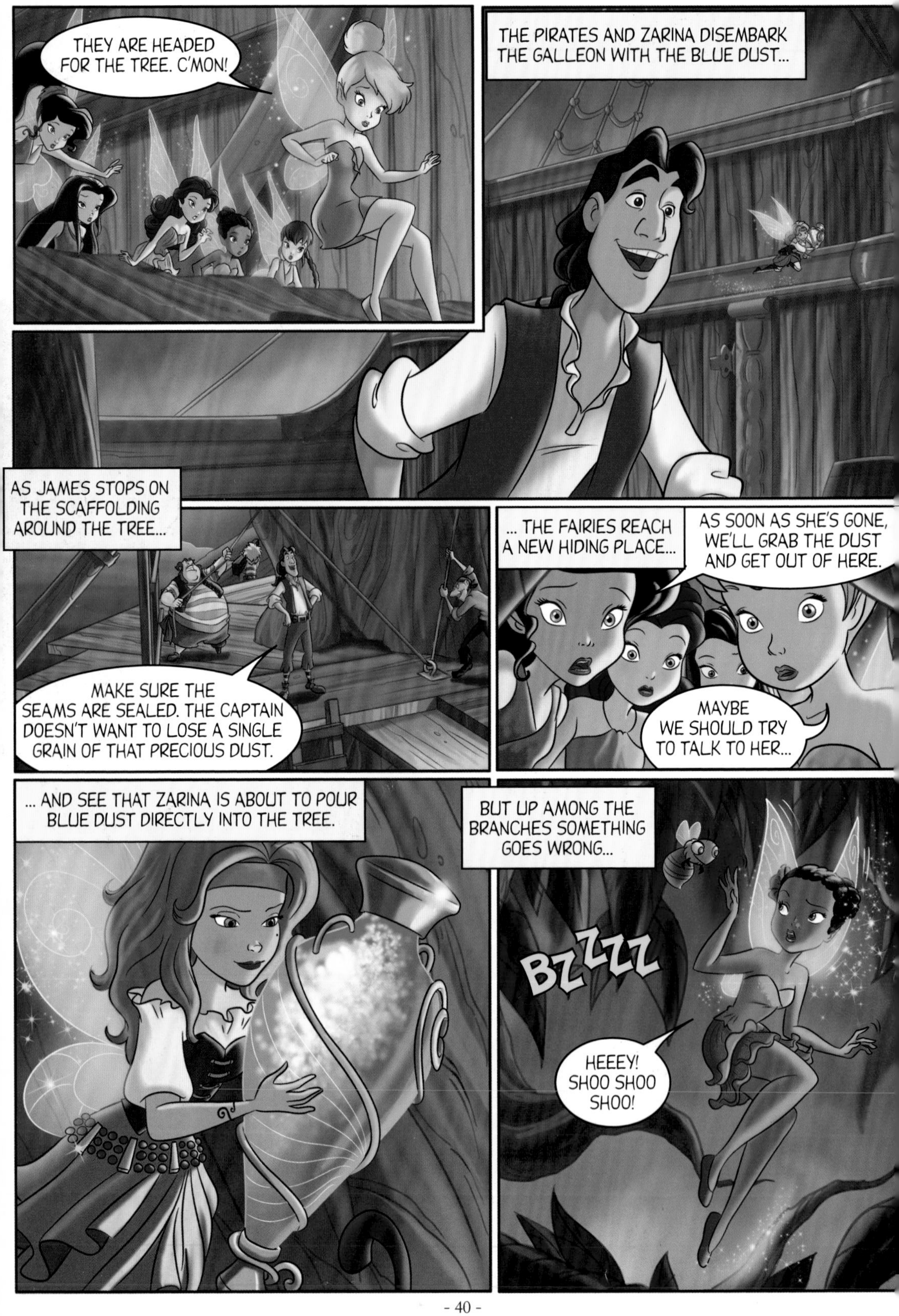
THEY ARE HEADED FOR THE TREE. C'MON!
THE PIRATES AND ZARINA DISEMBARK THE GALLEON WITH THE BLUE DUST...
AS JAMES STOPS ON THE SCAFFOLDING AROUND THE TREE...
MAKE SURE THE SEAMS ARE SEALED. THE CAPTAIN DOESN'T WANT TO LOSE A SINGLE GRAIN OF THAT PRECIOUS DUST.
... THE FAIRIES REACH A NEW HIDING PLACE...
AS SOON AS SHE'S GONE, WE'LL GRAB THE DUST AND GET OUT OF HERE.
MAYBE WE SHOULD TRY TO TALK TO HER...
... AND SEE THAT ZARINA IS ABOUT TO POUR BLUE DUST DIRECTLY INTO THE TREE.
BUT UP AMONG THE BRANCHES SOMETHING GOES WRONG...
BZZZZ
HEEEY! SHOO SHOO SHOO!

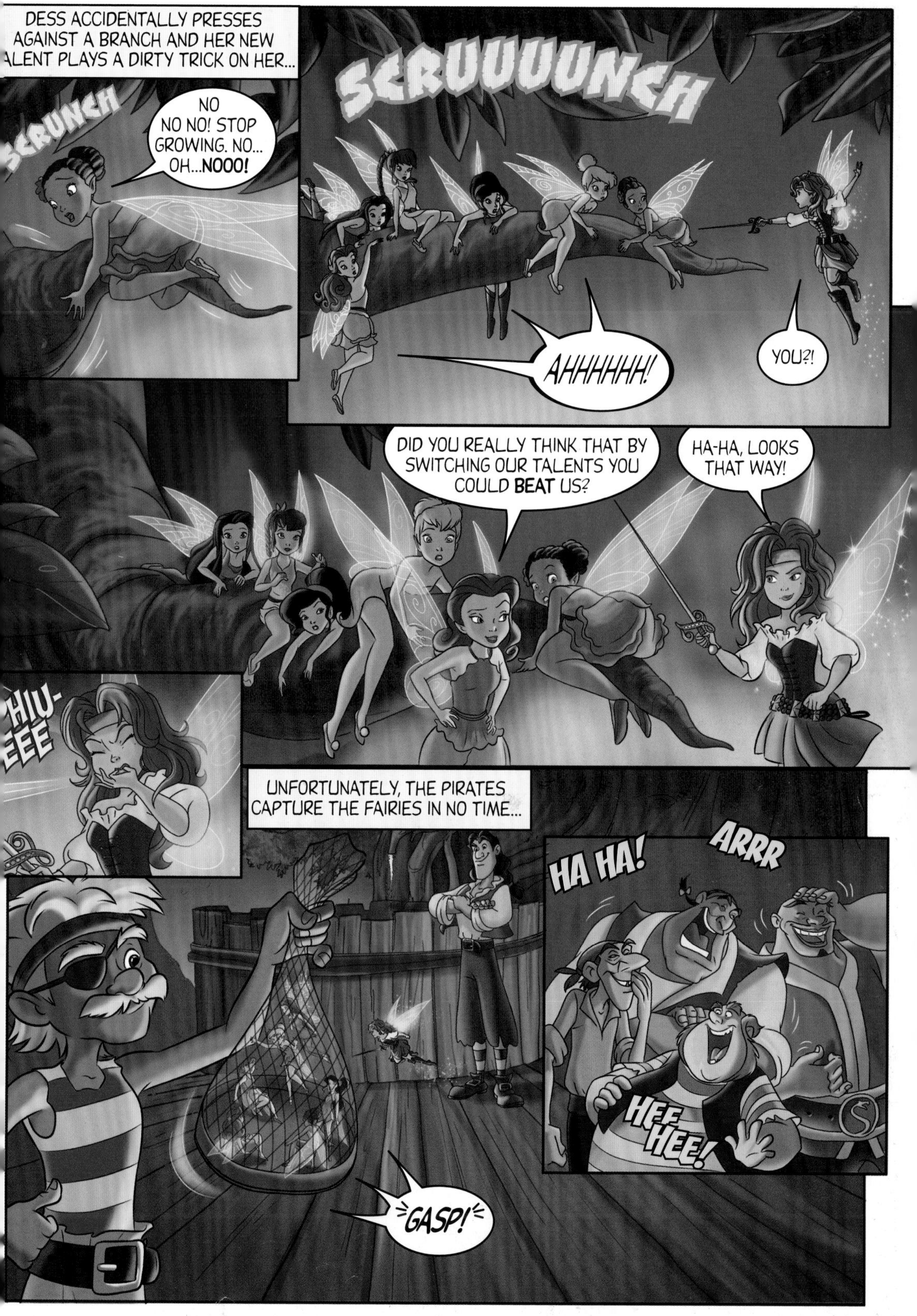
DESS ACCIDENTALLY PRESSES AGAINST A BRANCH AND HER NEW ALENT PLAYS A DIRTY TRICK ON HER...
SCRUNCH
NO NO NO! STOP GROWING. NO... OH...NOOO!
SCRUUUUUNCH
AHHHHHH!
YOU?!
DID YOU REALLY THINK THAT BY SWITCHING OUR TALENTS YOU COULD BEAT US?
HA-HA, LOOKS THAT WAY!
UNFORTUNATELY, THE PIRATES CAPTURE THE FAIRIES IN NO TIME...
HA HA!
ARRR
HEE HEE!
GASP!

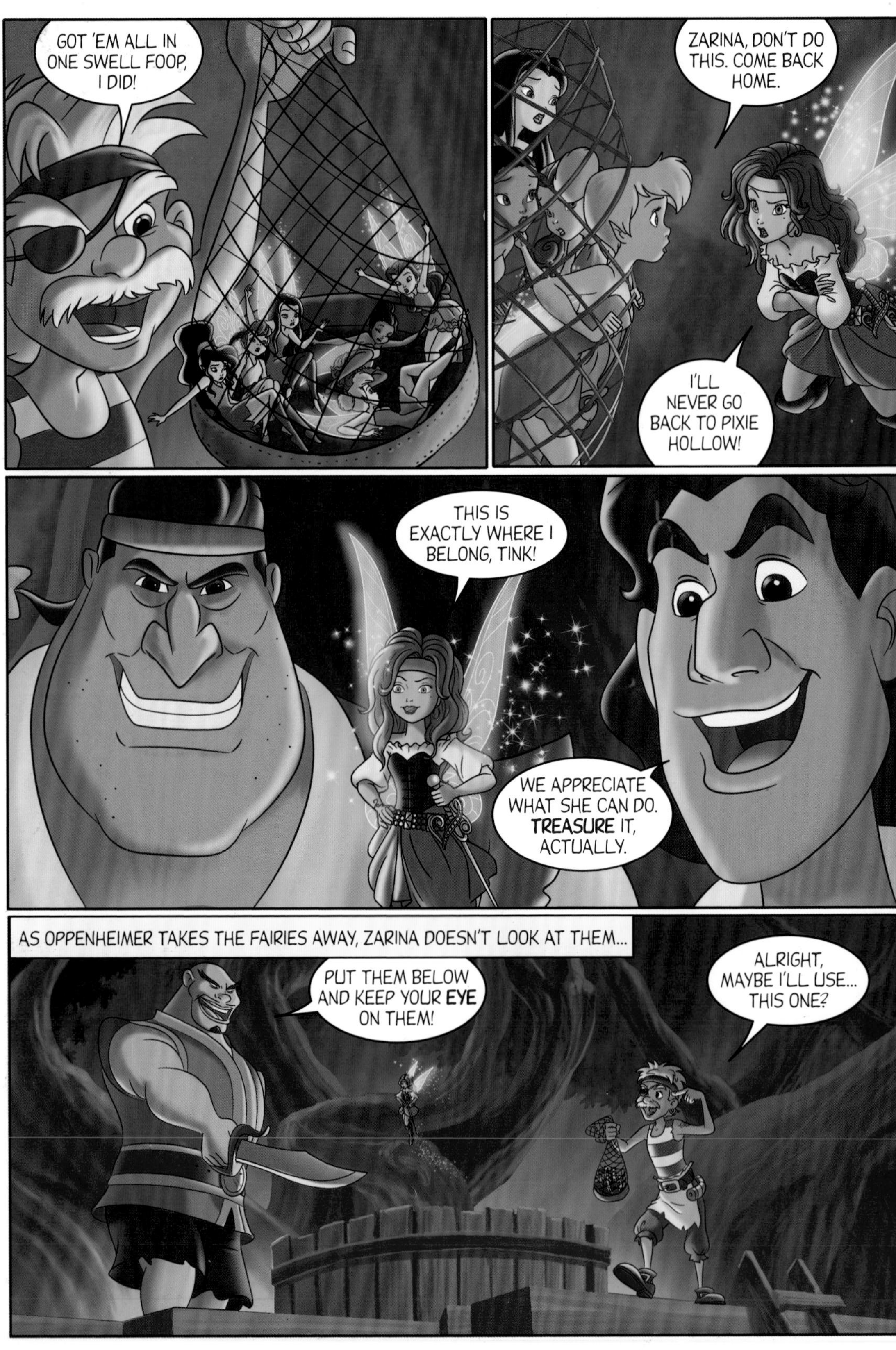
GOT 'EM ALL IN ONE SWELL FOOP, I DID!
ZARINA, DON'T DO THIS. COME BACK HOME.
I'LL NEVER GO BACK TO PIXIE HOLLOW!
THIS IS EXACTLY WHERE I BELONG, TINK!
WE APPRECIATE WHAT SHE CAN DO. **TREASURE** IT, ACTUALLY.
AS OPPENHEIMER TAKES THE FAIRIES AWAY, ZARINA DOESN'T LOOK AT THEM...
PUT THEM BELOW AND KEEP YOUR **EYE** ON THEM!
ALRIGHT, MAYBE I'LL USE... THIS ONE?

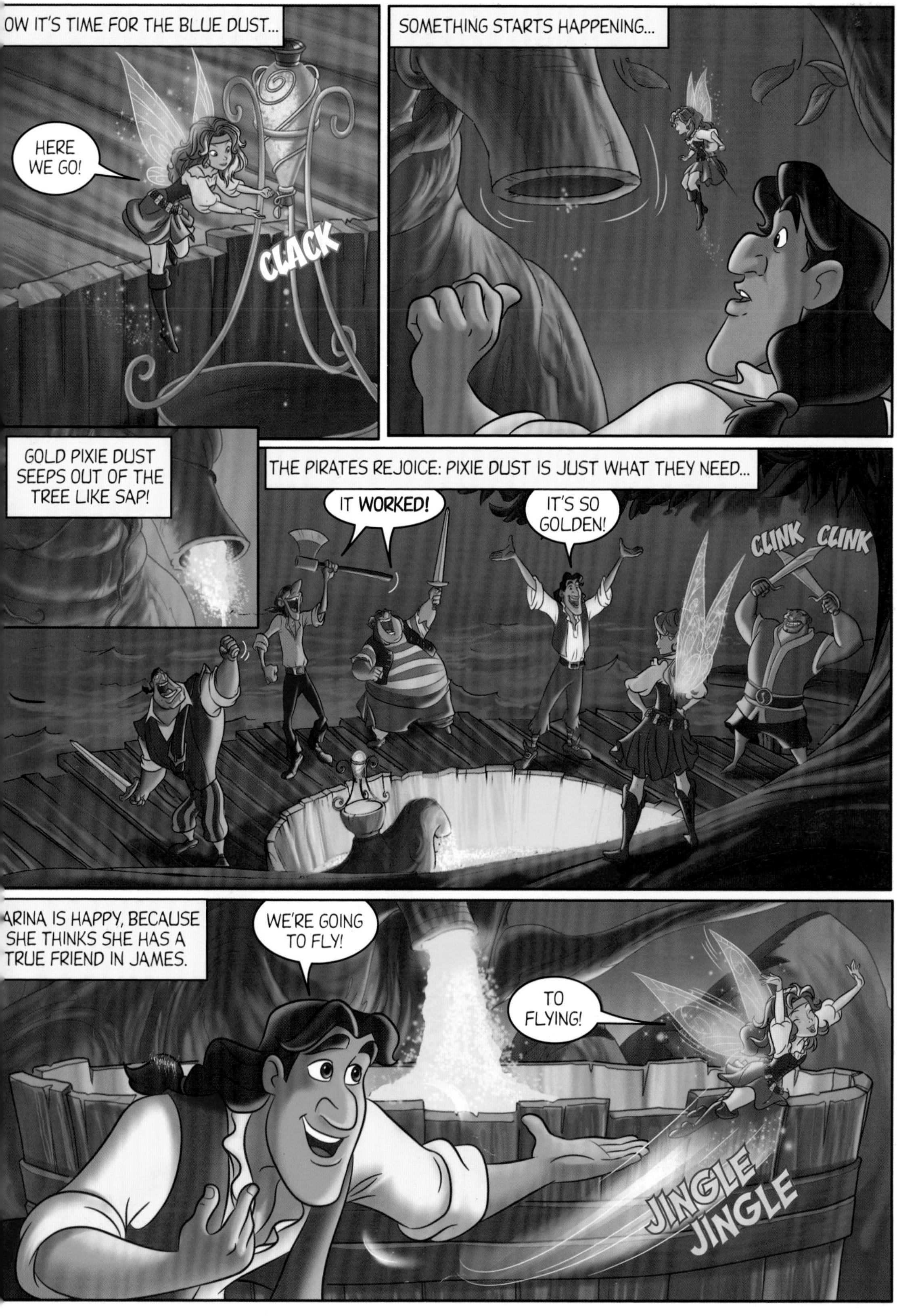
OW IT'S TIME FOR THE BLUE DUST...
HERE WE GO!
CLACK
SOMETHING STARTS HAPPENING...
GOLD PIXIE DUST SEEPS OUT OF THE TREE LIKE SAP!
THE PIRATES REJOICE: PIXIE DUST IS JUST WHAT THEY NEED...
IT WORKED!
IT'S SO GOLDEN!
CLINK CLINK
ARINA IS HAPPY, BECAUSE SHE THINKS SHE HAS A TRUE FRIEND IN JAMES.
WE'RE GOING TO FLY!
TO FLYING!
JINGLE JINGLE

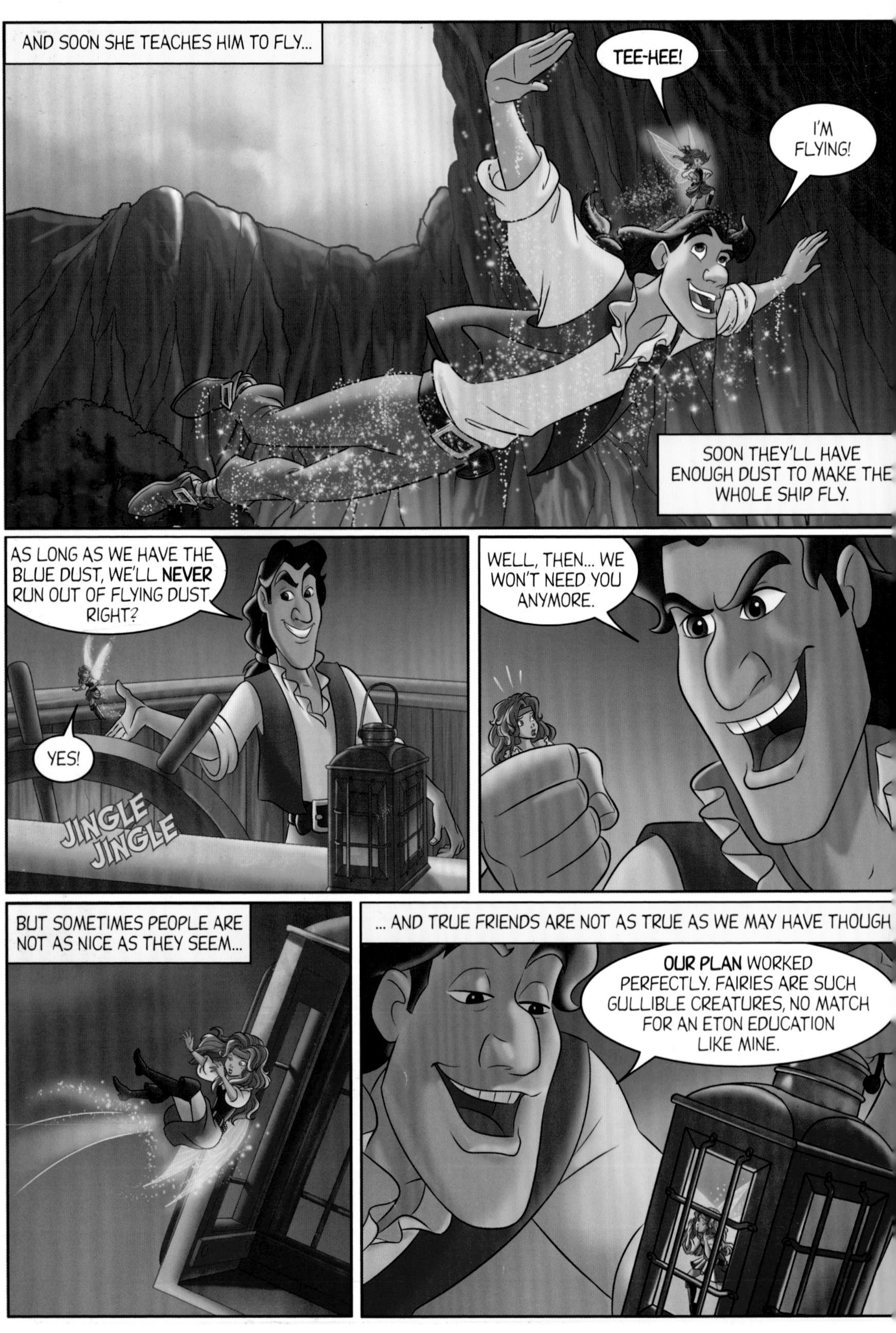
AND SOON SHE TEACHES HIM TO FLY...
TEE-HEE!
I'M FLYING!
SOON THEY'LL HAVE ENOUGH DUST TO MAKE THE WHOLE SHIP FLY.
AS LONG AS WE HAVE THE BLUE DUST, WE'LL **NEVER** RUN OUT OF FLYING DUST. RIGHT?
YES!
JINGLE JINGLE
WELL, THEN... WE WON'T NEED YOU ANYMORE.
BUT SOMETIMES PEOPLE ARE NOT AS NICE AS THEY SEEM...
... AND TRUE FRIENDS ARE NOT AS TRUE AS WE MAY HAVE THOUGH
**OUR PLAN** WORKED PERFECTLY. FAIRIES ARE SUCH GULLIBLE CREATURES, NO MATCH FOR AN ETON EDUCATION LIKE MINE.

THE POWER OF THE PIXIE DUST IS FINALLY OURS.

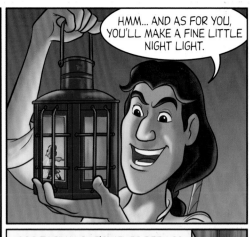

HMM... AND AS FOR YOU, YOU'LL MAKE A FINE LITTLE NIGHT LIGHT.

HOORAY!

HA-HA!

POOR ZARINA! SHE'S NEVER BEEN SO ASHAMED AND DEVASTATED.

IN THE CAPTAIN'S QUARTERS, SHE FINALLY REALIZES THAT **CAPTAIN** JAMES NEVER CARED ABOUT HER AT ALL...

SWOGGLE ME EYES! NOW THERE'S A SIGHT.

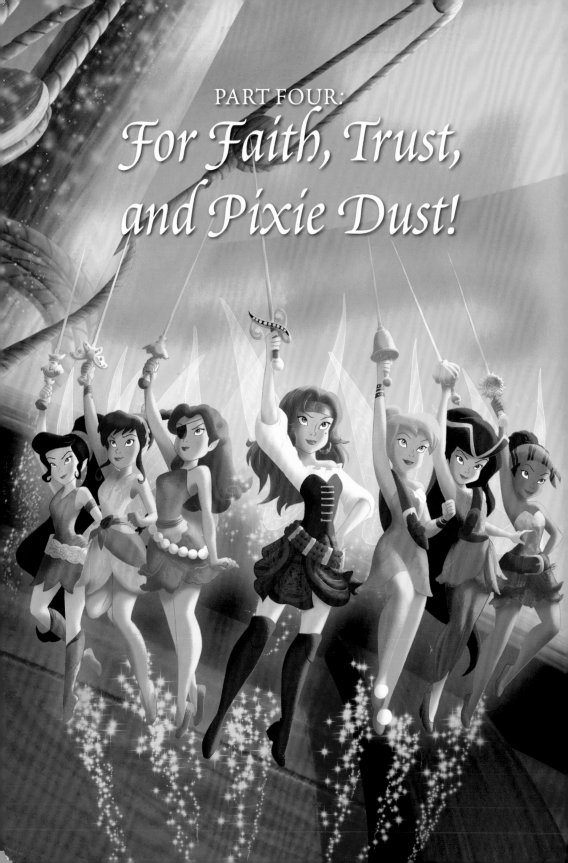

PART FOUR:
# For Faith, Trust, and Pixie Dust!

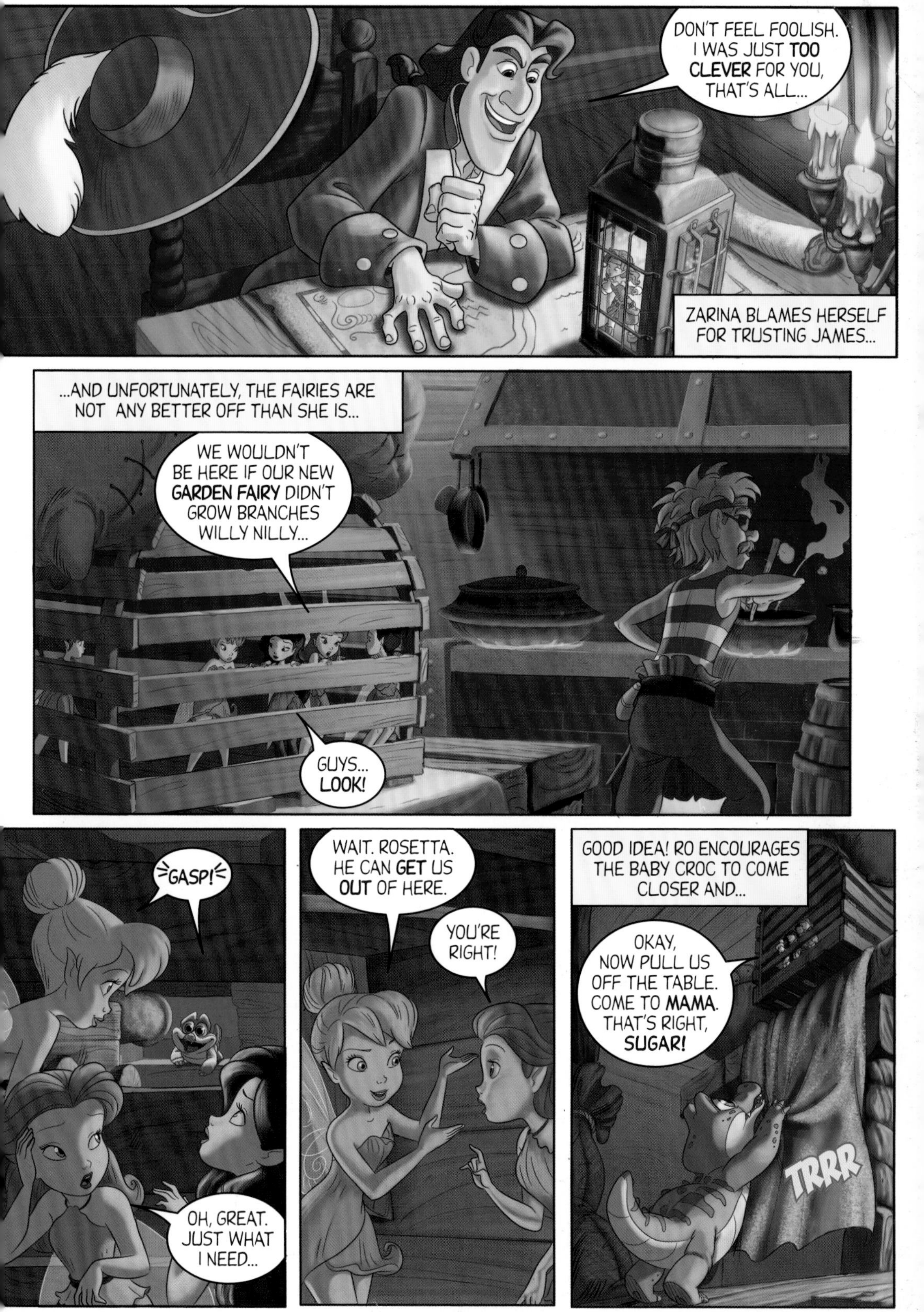
DON'T FEEL FOOLISH. I WAS JUST TOO CLEVER FOR YOU, THAT'S ALL...
ZARINA BLAMES HERSELF FOR TRUSTING JAMES...
...AND UNFORTUNATELY, THE FAIRIES ARE NOT ANY BETTER OFF THAN SHE IS...
WE WOULDN'T BE HERE IF OUR NEW GARDEN FAIRY DIDN'T GROW BRANCHES WILLY NILLY...
GUYS... LOOK!
GASP!
OH, GREAT. JUST WHAT I NEED...
WAIT. ROSETTA. HE CAN GET US OUT OF HERE.
YOU'RE RIGHT!
GOOD IDEA! RO ENCOURAGES THE BABY CROC TO COME CLOSER AND...
OKAY, NOW PULL US OFF THE TABLE. COME TO MAMA. THAT'S RIGHT, SUGAR!
TRRR

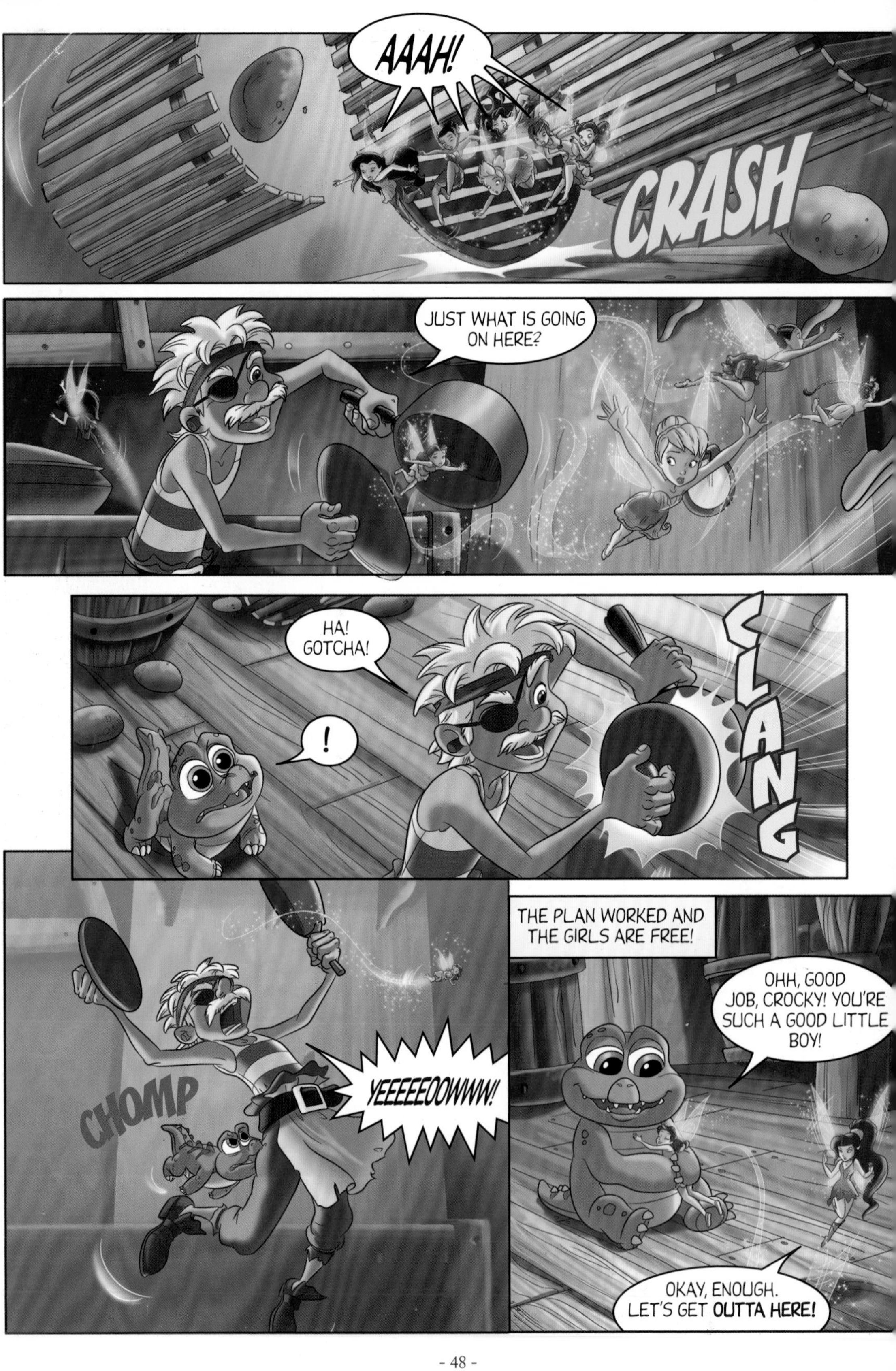
AAAH!
CRASH
JUST WHAT IS GOING ON HERE?
HA! GOTCHA!
!
CLANG
CHOMP
YEEEEEOOWWW!
THE PLAN WORKED AND THE GIRLS ARE FREE!
OHH, GOOD JOB, CROCKY! YOU'RE SUCH A GOOD LITTLE BOY!
OKAY, ENOUGH. LET'S GET **OUTTA HERE!**

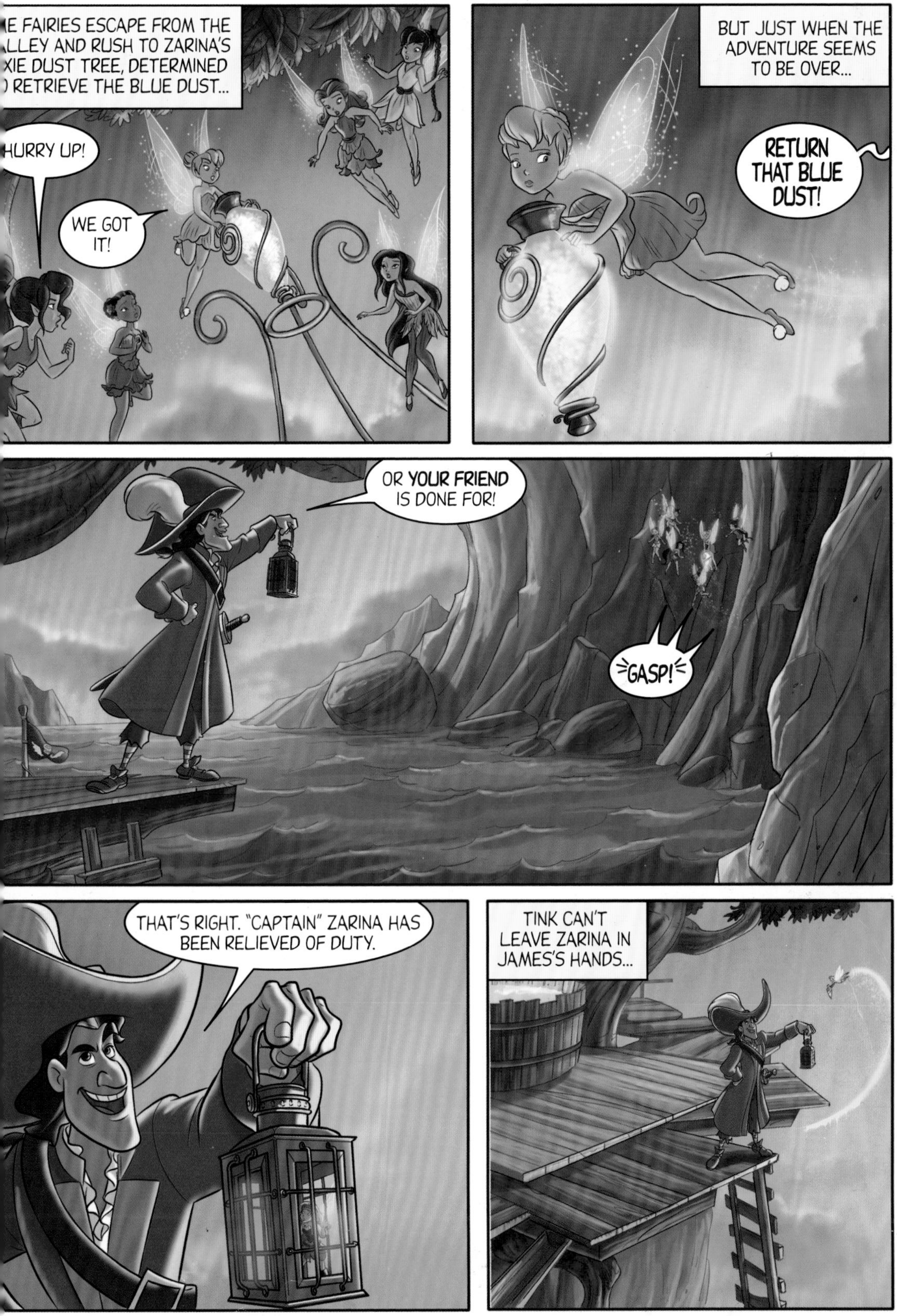
E FAIRIES ESCAPE FROM THE
LLEY AND RUSH TO ZARINA'S
XIE DUST TREE, DETERMINED
RETRIEVE THE BLUE DUST...
HURRY UP!
WE GOT IT!
BUT JUST WHEN THE ADVENTURE SEEMS TO BE OVER...
RETURN THAT BLUE DUST!
OR YOUR FRIEND IS DONE FOR!
GASP!
THAT'S RIGHT. "CAPTAIN" ZARINA HAS BEEN RELIEVED OF DUTY.
TINK CAN'T LEAVE ZARINA IN JAMES'S HANDS...

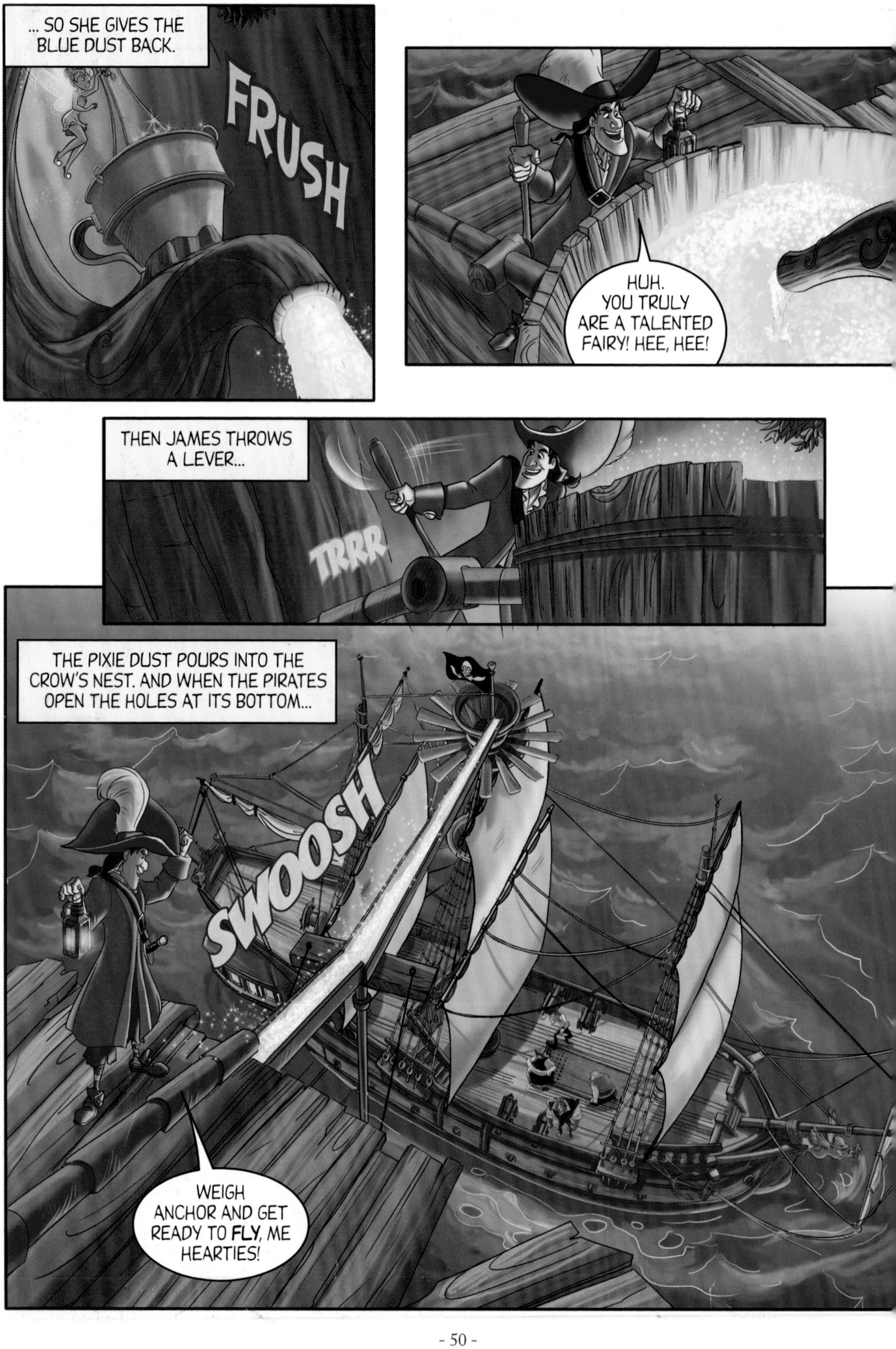
... SO SHE GIVES THE BLUE DUST BACK.
FRUSH
HUH. YOU TRULY ARE A TALENTED FAIRY! HEE, HEE!
THEN JAMES THROWS A LEVER...
TRRR
THE PIXIE DUST POURS INTO THE CROW'S NEST. AND WHEN THE PIRATES OPEN THE HOLES AT ITS BOTTOM...
SWOOSH
WEIGH ANCHOR AND GET READY TO FLY, ME HEARTIES!

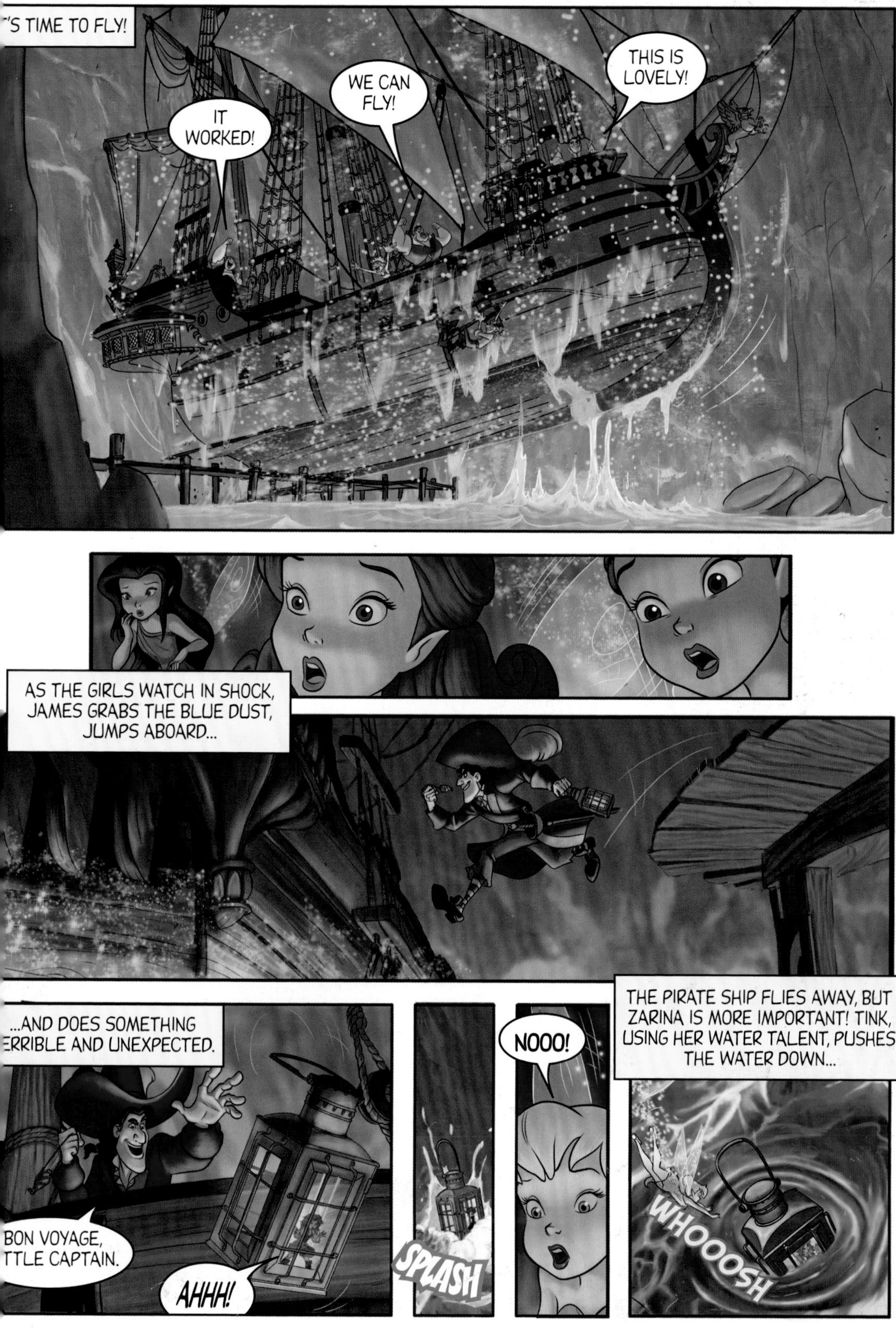
'S TIME TO FLY!
IT WORKED!
WE CAN FLY!
THIS IS LOVELY!
AS THE GIRLS WATCH IN SHOCK, JAMES GRABS THE BLUE DUST, JUMPS ABOARD...
...AND DOES SOMETHING
ERRIBLE AND UNEXPECTED.
BON VOYAGE, TTLE CAPTAIN.
AHHH!
SPLASH
NOOO!
THE PIRATE SHIP FLIES AWAY, BUT ZARINA IS MORE IMPORTANT! TINK, USING HER WATER TALENT, PUSHES THE WATER DOWN...
WHOOOSH

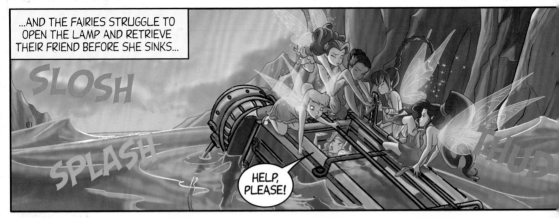

...AND THE FAIRIES STRUGGLE TO OPEN THE LAMP AND RETRIEVE THEIR FRIEND BEFORE SHE SINKS...

SLOSH

SPLASH

THUD

HELP, PLEASE!

GASP!

CLACK

THE FAIRIES FLY OVER TO THE SAFETY OF THE ROCKS, AND ZARINA IS HUMBLY GRATEFUL.

YOU SAVED ME... WHY?

LET'S JUST SAY WE'RE OFFERING YOU **QUARTER!**

I'M SO SORRY.

WE CAN STILL GET THE BLUE DUST BACK. BUT WE HAVE TO DO IT BEFORE THEY PASS THE SECOND STAR, OR THEY'LL BE GONE FOREVER.

THEN LET'S STOP THEM BEFORE THEY GET THERE.

CAPTAIN.

ZARINA AND THE FAIRIES REACH THE FLYING GALLEON AS IT GETS CLOSER TO THE SECOND STAR...

YOU GUYS TURN THIS SHIP AROUND. I'M GETTING BACK THAT BLUE DUST!

RIGHT!

NOW IT'S TIME TO GET THE BLUE DUST BACK!

SMASH

AND TO START THE BATTLE!

WHAM

HUH?!?

FAIRIES! FAIRIES! IT'S THE FAIRIES!

BUT SOON, DESPITE THEIR GREAT EFFORTS, THE PIRATES MANAGE TO TRAP THE FAIRIES INSIDE A PIECE OF SAIL.

TWACK

ZARINA, HOWEVER, CARRIES OUT HER OWN PLAN...

Swish

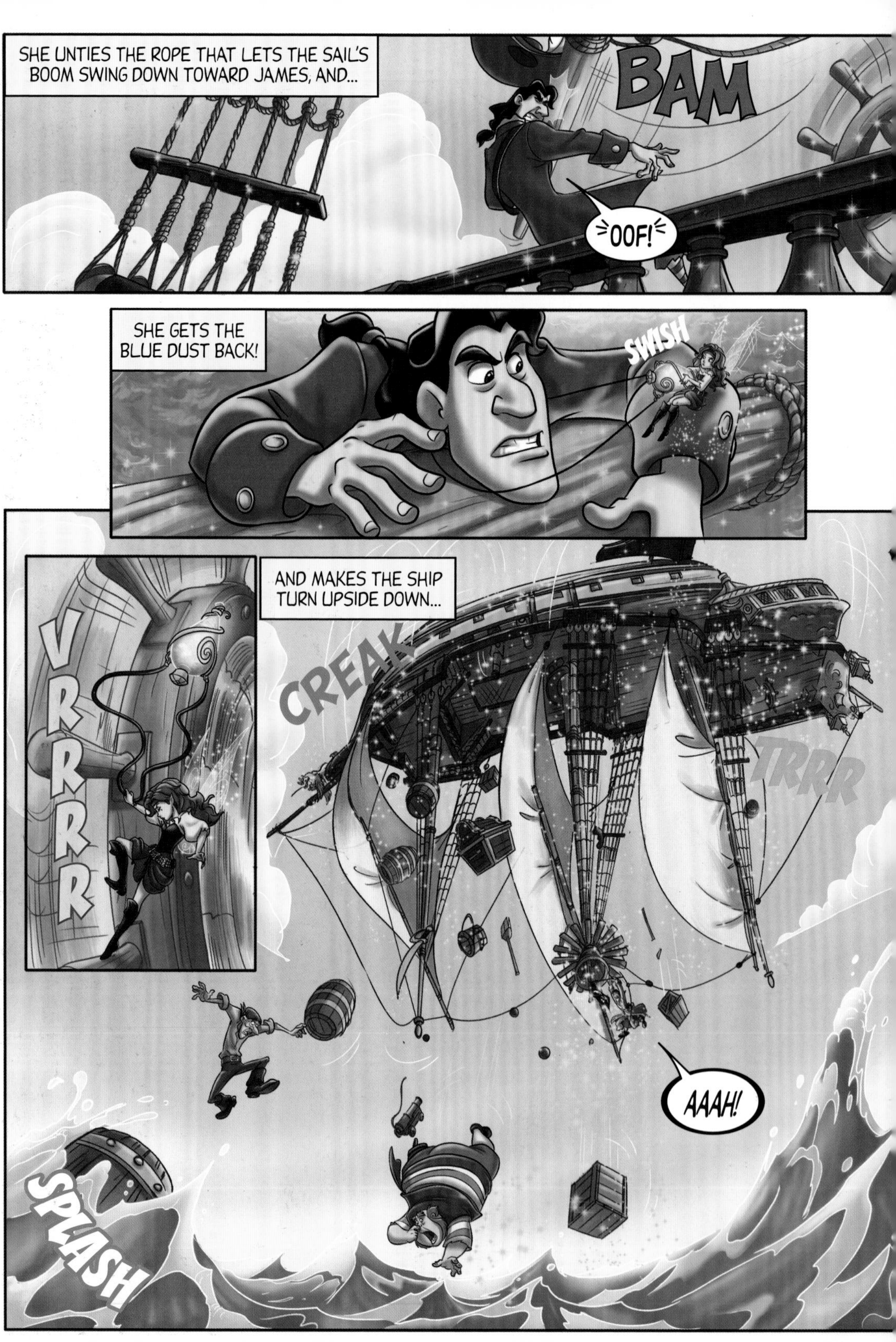
SHE UNTIES THE ROPE THAT LETS THE SAIL'S BOOM SWING DOWN TOWARD JAMES, AND...
BAM
OOF!
SHE GETS THE BLUE DUST BACK!
SWISH
AND MAKES THE SHIP TURN UPSIDE DOWN...
VRRRR
CREAK
TRRR
AAAH!
SPLASH

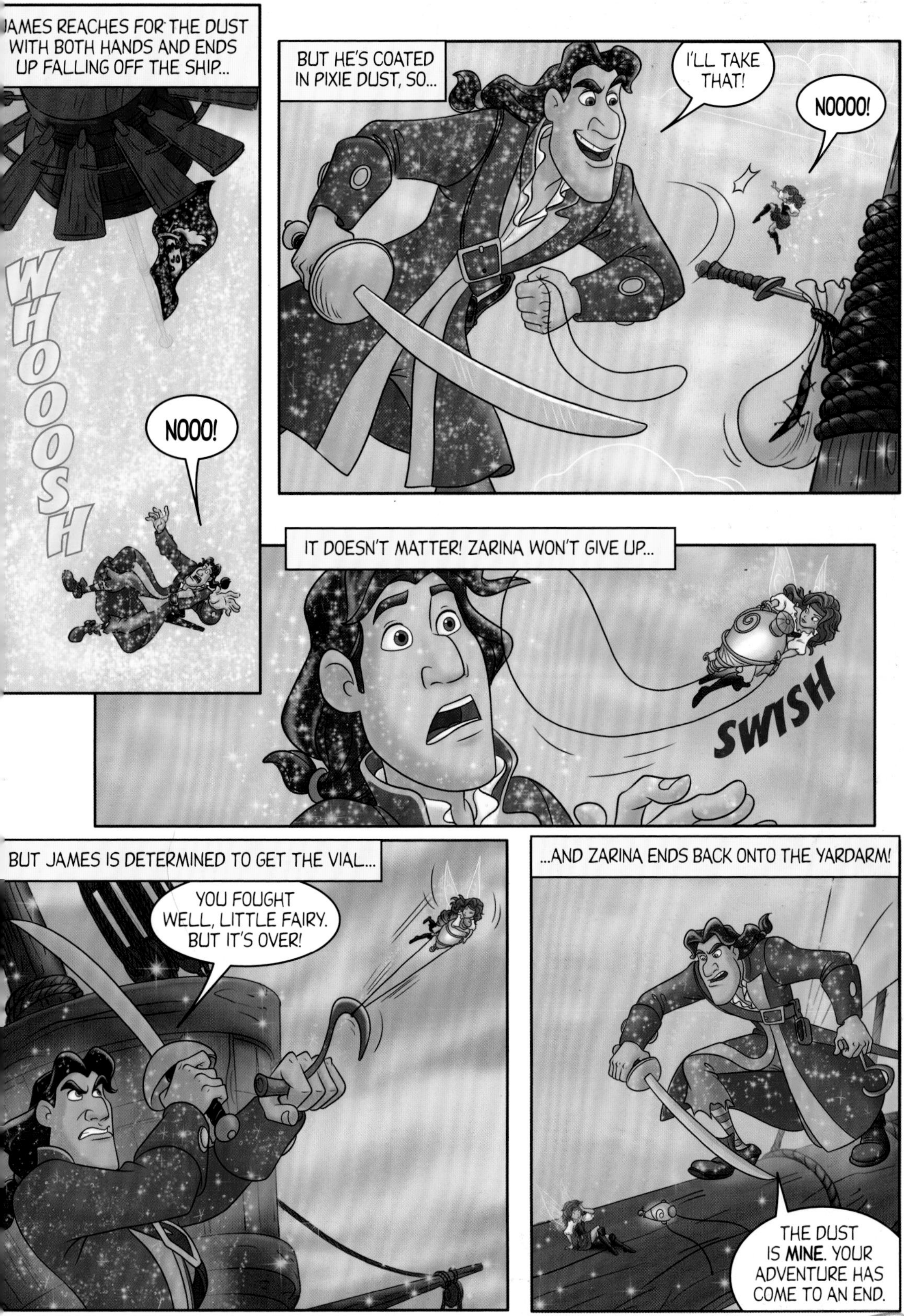
JAMES REACHES FOR THE DUST WITH BOTH HANDS AND ENDS UP FALLING OFF THE SHIP...
WHOOOOSH
NOOO!
BUT HE'S COATED IN PIXIE DUST, SO...
I'LL TAKE THAT!
NOOOO!
IT DOESN'T MATTER! ZARINA WON'T GIVE UP...
SWISH
BUT JAMES IS DETERMINED TO GET THE VIAL...
YOU FOUGHT WELL, LITTLE FAIRY. BUT IT'S OVER!
...AND ZARINA ENDS BACK ONTO THE YARDARM!
THE DUST IS **MINE**. YOUR ADVENTURE HAS COME TO AN END.

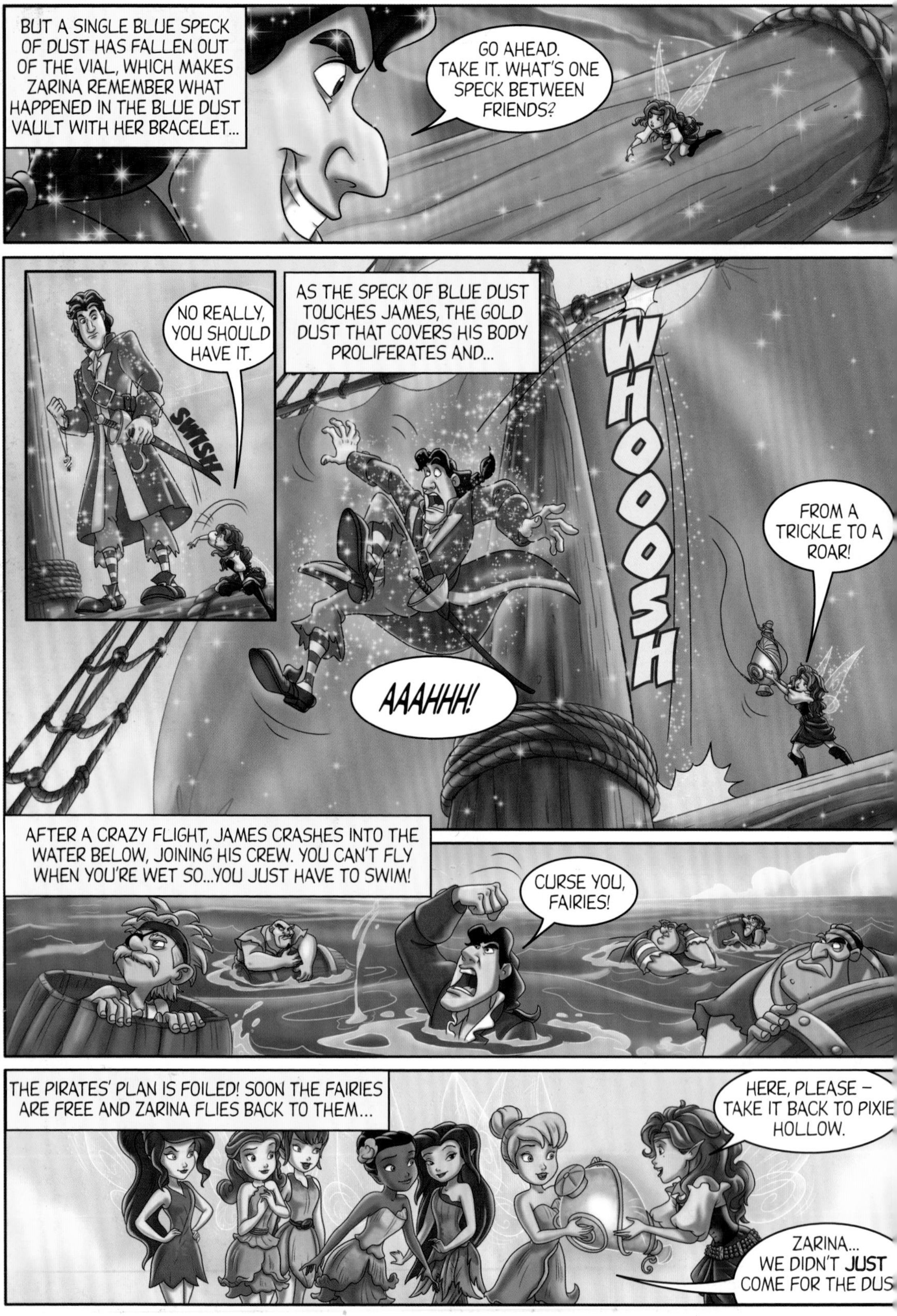

BUT A SINGLE BLUE SPECK OF DUST HAS FALLEN OUT OF THE VIAL, WHICH MAKES ZARINA REMEMBER WHAT HAPPENED IN THE BLUE DUST VAULT WITH HER BRACELET...
GO AHEAD. TAKE IT. WHAT'S ONE SPECK BETWEEN FRIENDS?
NO REALLY, YOU SHOULD HAVE IT.
SWISH
AS THE SPECK OF BLUE DUST TOUCHES JAMES, THE GOLD DUST THAT COVERS HIS BODY PROLIFERATES AND...
WHOOOOSH
FROM A TRICKLE TO A ROAR!
AAAHHH!
AFTER A CRAZY FLIGHT, JAMES CRASHES INTO THE WATER BELOW, JOINING HIS CREW. YOU CAN'T FLY WHEN YOU'RE WET SO...YOU JUST HAVE TO SWIM!
CURSE YOU, FAIRIES!
THE PIRATES' PLAN IS FOILED! SOON THE FAIRIES ARE FREE AND ZARINA FLIES BACK TO THEM...
HERE, PLEASE – TAKE IT BACK TO PIXIE HOLLOW.
ZARINA... WE DIDN'T **JUST** COME FOR THE DUS

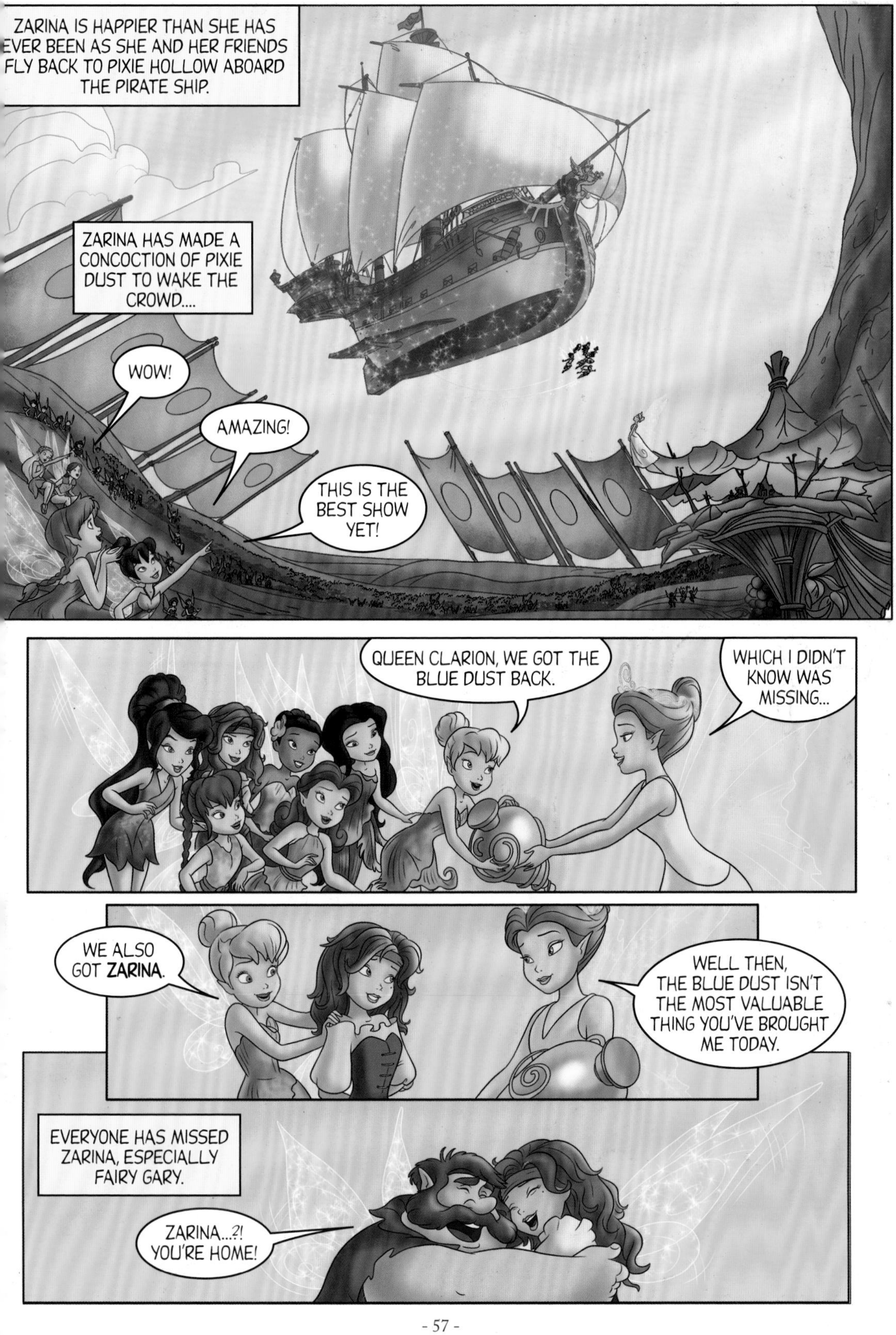
ZARINA IS HAPPIER THAN SHE HAS EVER BEEN AS SHE AND HER FRIENDS FLY BACK TO PIXIE HOLLOW ABOARD THE PIRATE SHIP.
ZARINA HAS MADE A CONCOCTION OF PIXIE DUST TO WAKE THE CROWD....
WOW!
AMAZING!
THIS IS THE BEST SHOW YET!
QUEEN CLARION, WE GOT THE BLUE DUST BACK.
WHICH I DIDN'T KNOW WAS MISSING...
WE ALSO GOT **ZARINA**.
WELL THEN, THE BLUE DUST ISN'T THE MOST VALUABLE THING YOU'VE BROUGHT ME TODAY.
EVERYONE HAS MISSED ZARINA, ESPECIALLY FAIRY GARY.
ZARINA...?! YOU'RE HOME!

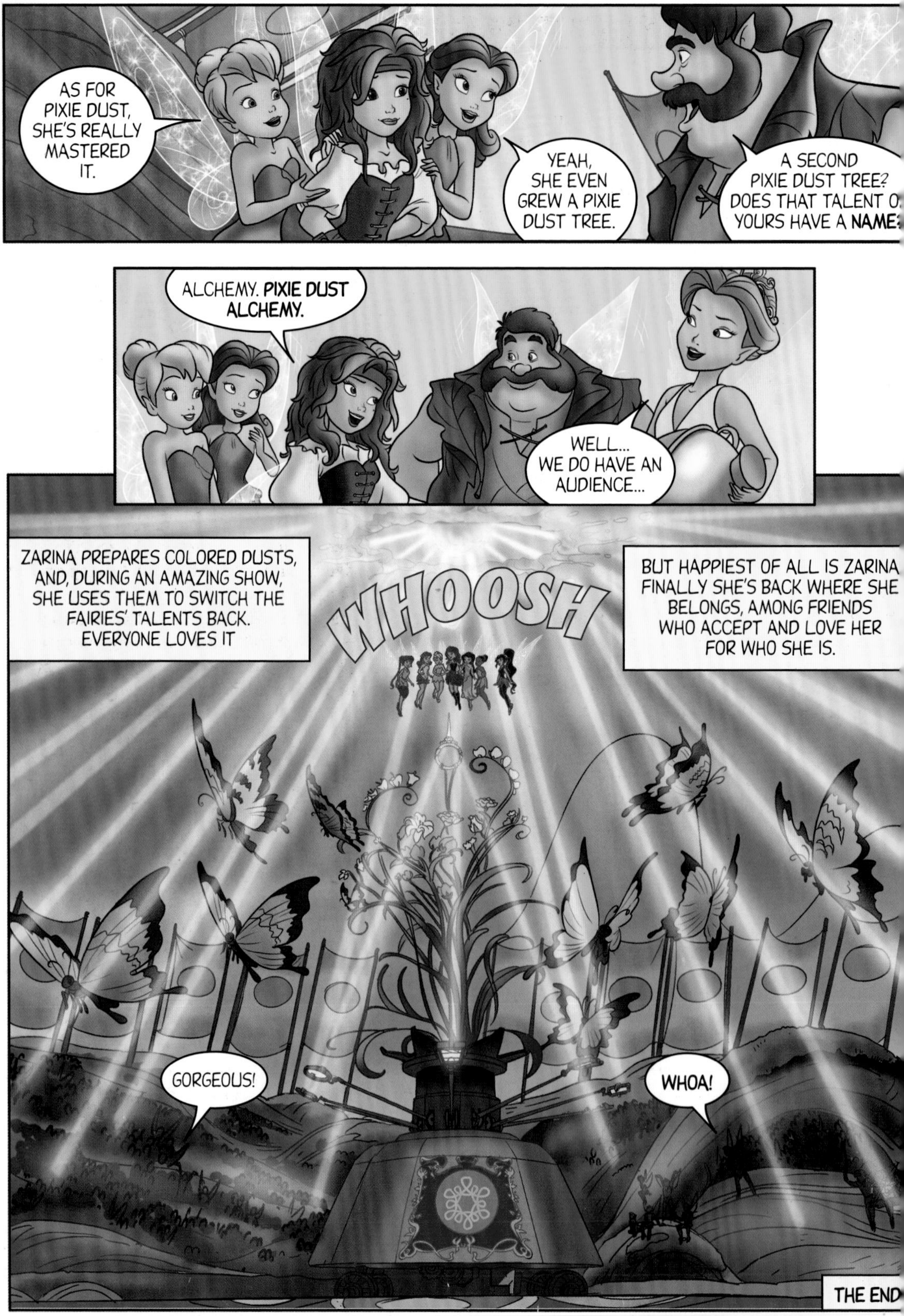
AS FOR PIXIE DUST, SHE'S REALLY MASTERED IT.
YEAH, SHE EVEN GREW A PIXIE DUST TREE.
A SECOND PIXIE DUST TREE? DOES THAT TALENT O YOURS HAVE A NAME
ALCHEMY. PIXIE DUST ALCHEMY.
WELL... WE DO HAVE AN AUDIENCE...
ZARINA PREPARES COLORED DUSTS, AND, DURING AN AMAZING SHOW, SHE USES THEM TO SWITCH THE FAIRIES' TALENTS BACK. EVERYONE LOVES IT
WHOOSH
BUT HAPPIEST OF ALL IS ZARINA FINALLY SHE'S BACK WHERE SHE BELONGS, AMONG FRIENDS WHO ACCEPT AND LOVE HER FOR WHO SHE IS.
GORGEOUS!
WHOA!
THE END

# WATCH OUT FOR PAPERCUTZ™

ARRR! Welcome to the sea-faring sixteenth DISNEY FAIRIES graphic novel from Papercutz, those bilge rats dedicated to publishing great graphic novels for all ages. I'm Jim Salicrup, the Captain, er, Editor-in-Chief, and I'm here to share a thought or two and make a BIG ANNOUNCEMENT! So pay close attention, ya land-lubbers!

"Tinker Bell and the Pirate Fairy" may be one of the most thought-provoking DISNEY FAIRIES graphic novels we've published yet! For example, is Zarina a good fairy or a bad fairy? That's a tough question to answer. On one hand, she didn't follow the rules. She thought certainly Tinker Bell would understand—Tink's been known to break a rule or two. On the other hand, she was merely trying to explore the powers of the pixie dust. Many a great discovery was made by folks unafraid to go where no man, or fairy, had gone before.

When Zarina was misunderstood by Tinker Bell, it really hurt her feelings. She thought no one understood her, until she met James the pirate (he really looks familiar, doesn't he?). Sometimes, when we're really hurt emotionally, we're so desperate to find friends we'll look the other way and ignore certain warning signs. In Zarina's case, she fell in with a bad crowd—pirates! She thought she had new friends, but you saw what happened. This should be a lesson to all of us, to not be so quick to abandon our friends when our feelings are hurt. Our friends, just like everyone else, are only human, even if they're fairies, and can make mistakes. Better to forgive than run away.

Speaking of friends, there's another Papercutz graphic novel series that's all about family and friendship—it's called ERNEST & REBECCA. Rebecca is six-and-a-half years old girl, and her best friend is a microbe. You know—a germ. Well, that may not be normal, but what is these days? In the latest ERNEST & REBECCA graphic novel, #5 "The School of Nonsense," a bad virus is causing many of the students in Rebecca's school to get sick.

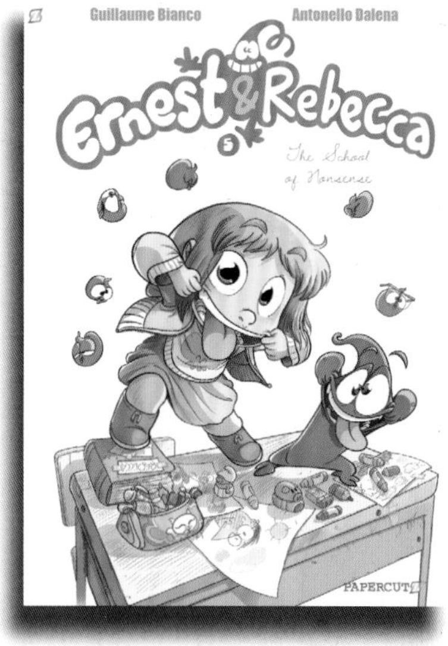
Guillaume Bianco
Antonello Dalena
Ernest & Rebecca
5
The School of Nonsense
PAPERCUTZ

ERNEST & REBECCA © Editions Du Lombard

Fortunately, Ernest hopes to protect the remaining healthy students. In the midst of all this drama, Rebecca's teacher tries to keep everyone's spirits up by breaking a few rules—just like Zarina! There's a few pages from ERNEST & REBECCA following after the next two pages. We hope you enjoy them. To get the full story, you'll have to track down the ERNEST & REBECCA #5 graphic novel. If it's not at your favorite bookseller, just ask for it, and they should be able to order it for you.

And now for our BIG ANNOUNCEMENT! One of the greatest, longest running comics series of all time will soon be returning. It's WALT DISNEY'S COMICS AND STORIES and Papercutz is proud to be publishing this classic title! Don't miss the first Papercutz WALT DISNEY'S COMIC AND STORIES graphic novel, featuring Disney's Planes! Future graphic novels will feature Mickey Mouse, Minnie Mouse, Daisy Duck, and many more! You may never know who will be popping up next in WALT DISNEY'S COMICS AND STORIES! This is a dream come true for me to get to edit such an important, well-respected, legendary comics title. Just goes to show what's possible, when you believe in "faith, trust, and pixie dust"!

Thanks,

Jim

## STAY IN TOUCH!

| | |
|---|---|
| EMAIL: | salicrup@papercutz.com |
| WEB: | papercutz.com |
| TWITTER: | @papercutzgn |
| FACEBOOK: | PAPERCUTZGRAPHICNOVELS |
| REGULAR MAIL: | Papercutz, 160 Broadway, Suite 700, East Wing, New York, NY 10038 |

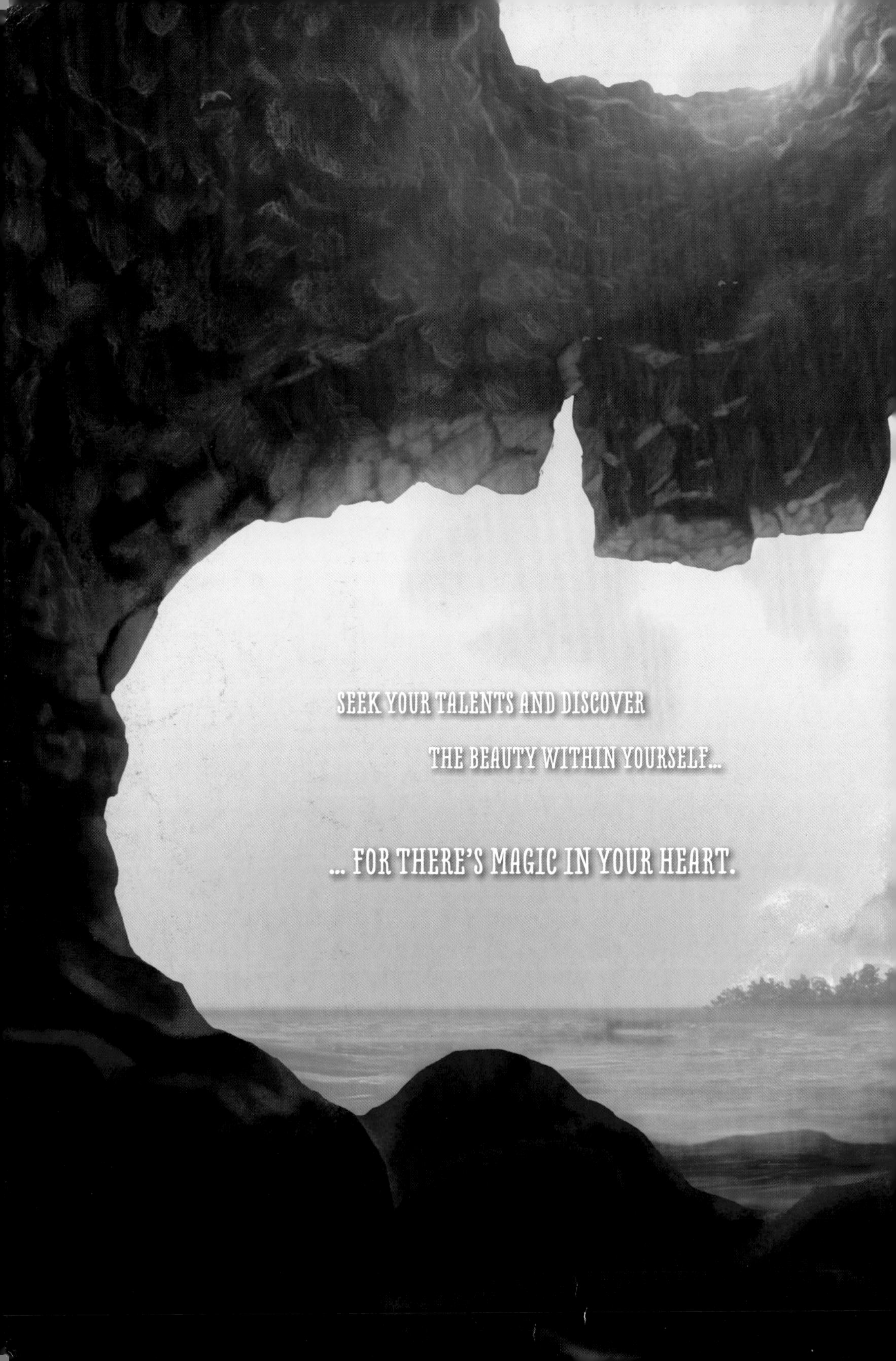
SEEK YOUR TALENTS AND DISCOVER
THE BEAUTY WITHIN YOURSELF...
... FOR THERE'S MAGIC IN YOUR HEART.

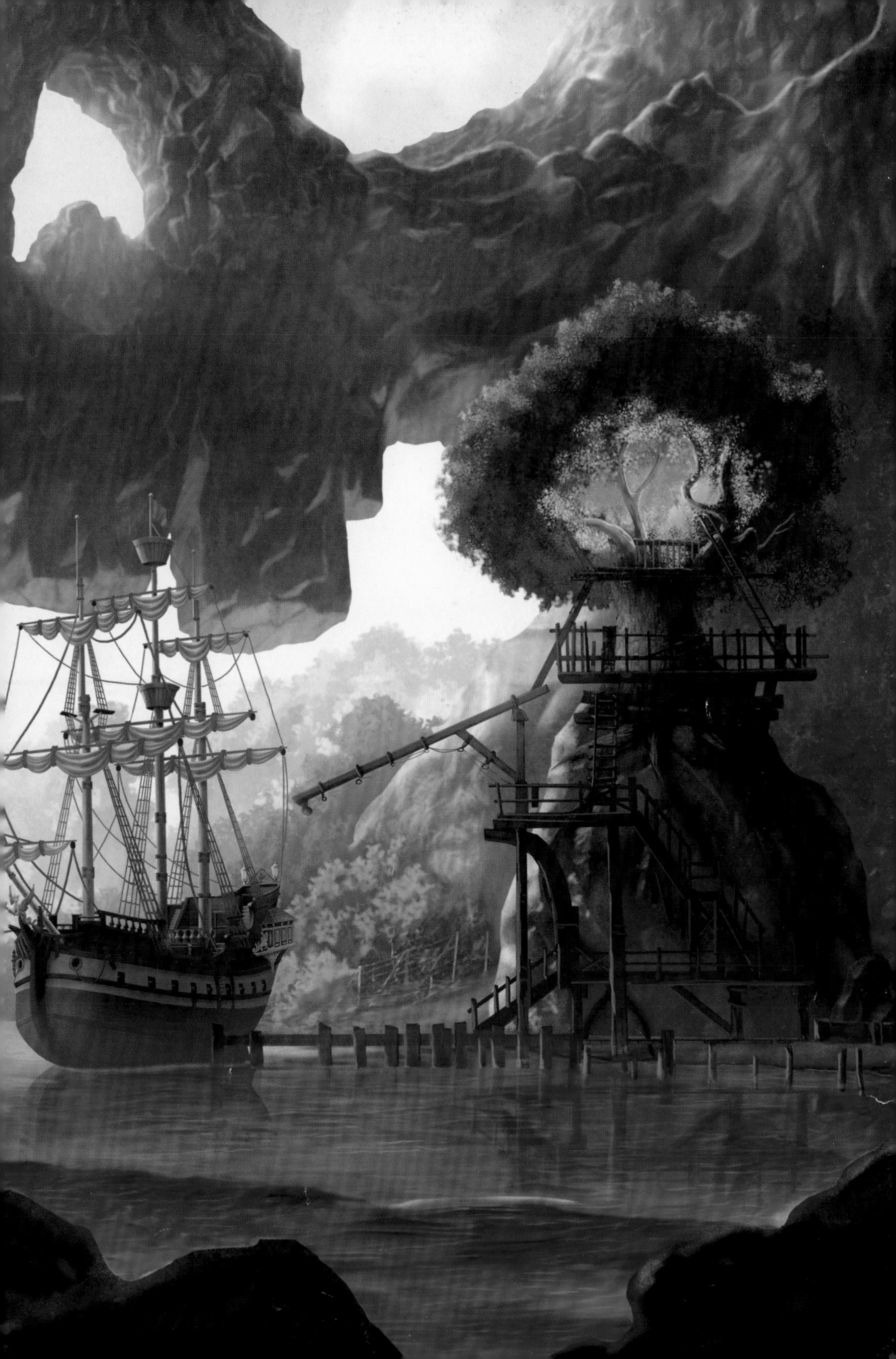

A Special Excerpt from ERNEST & REBECCA #5 “The School of Nonsense”...

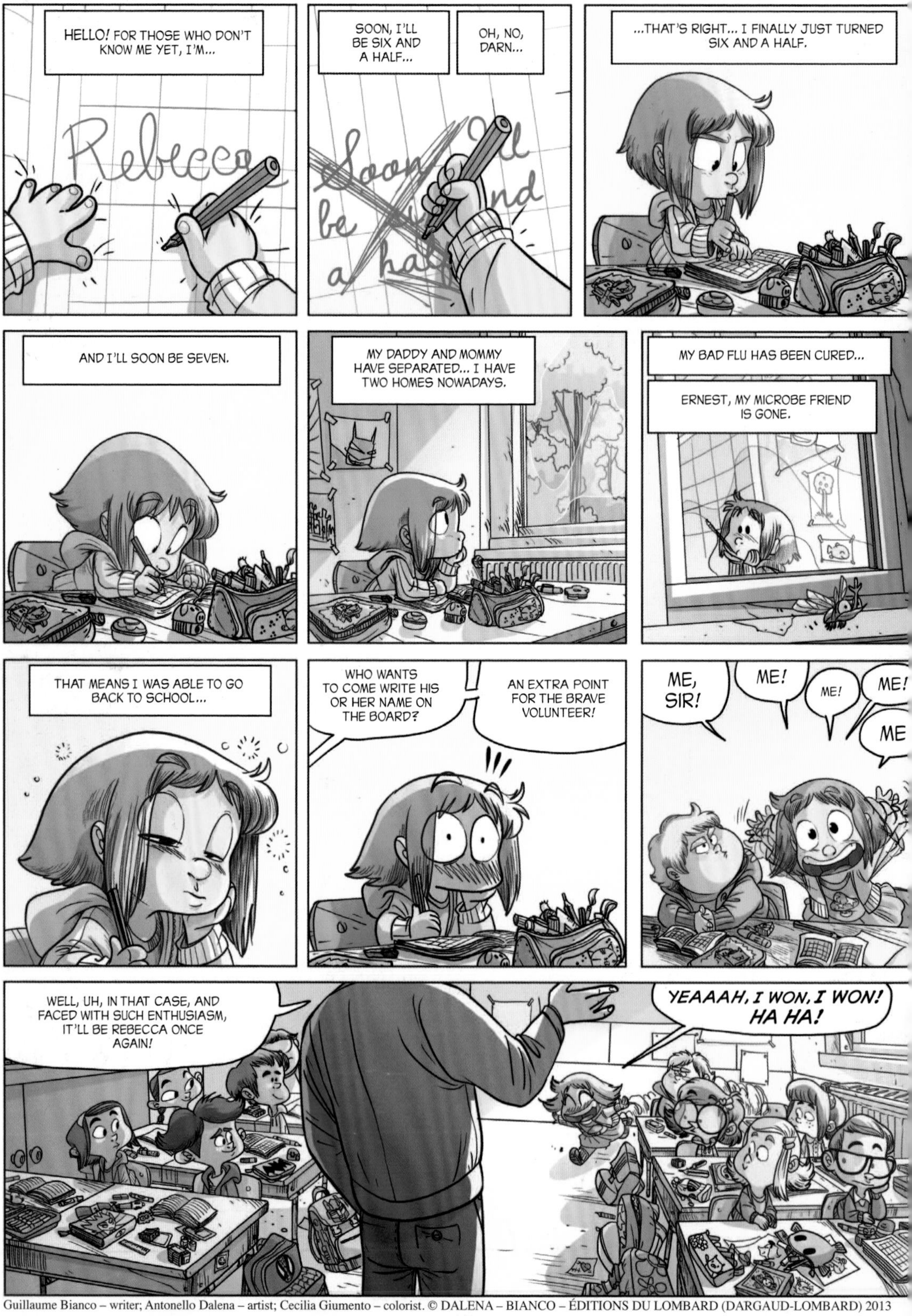
HELLO! FOR THOSE WHO DON'T KNOW ME YET, I'M...
Rebecca
SOON, I'LL BE SIX AND A HALF...
OH, NO, DARN...
...THAT'S RIGHT... I FINALLY JUST TURNED SIX AND A HALF.
AND I'LL SOON BE SEVEN.
MY DADDY AND MOMMY HAVE SEPARATED... I HAVE TWO HOMES NOWADAYS.
MY BAD FLU HAS BEEN CURED...
ERNEST, MY MICROBE FRIEND IS GONE.
THAT MEANS I WAS ABLE TO GO BACK TO SCHOOL...
WHO WANTS TO COME WRITE HIS OR HER NAME ON THE BOARD?
AN EXTRA POINT FOR THE BRAVE VOLUNTEER!
ME, SIR!
ME!
ME!
ME!
ME
WELL, UH, IN THAT CASE, AND FACED WITH SUCH ENTHUSIASM, IT'LL BE REBECCA ONCE AGAIN!
YEAAAH, I WON, I WON! HA HA!

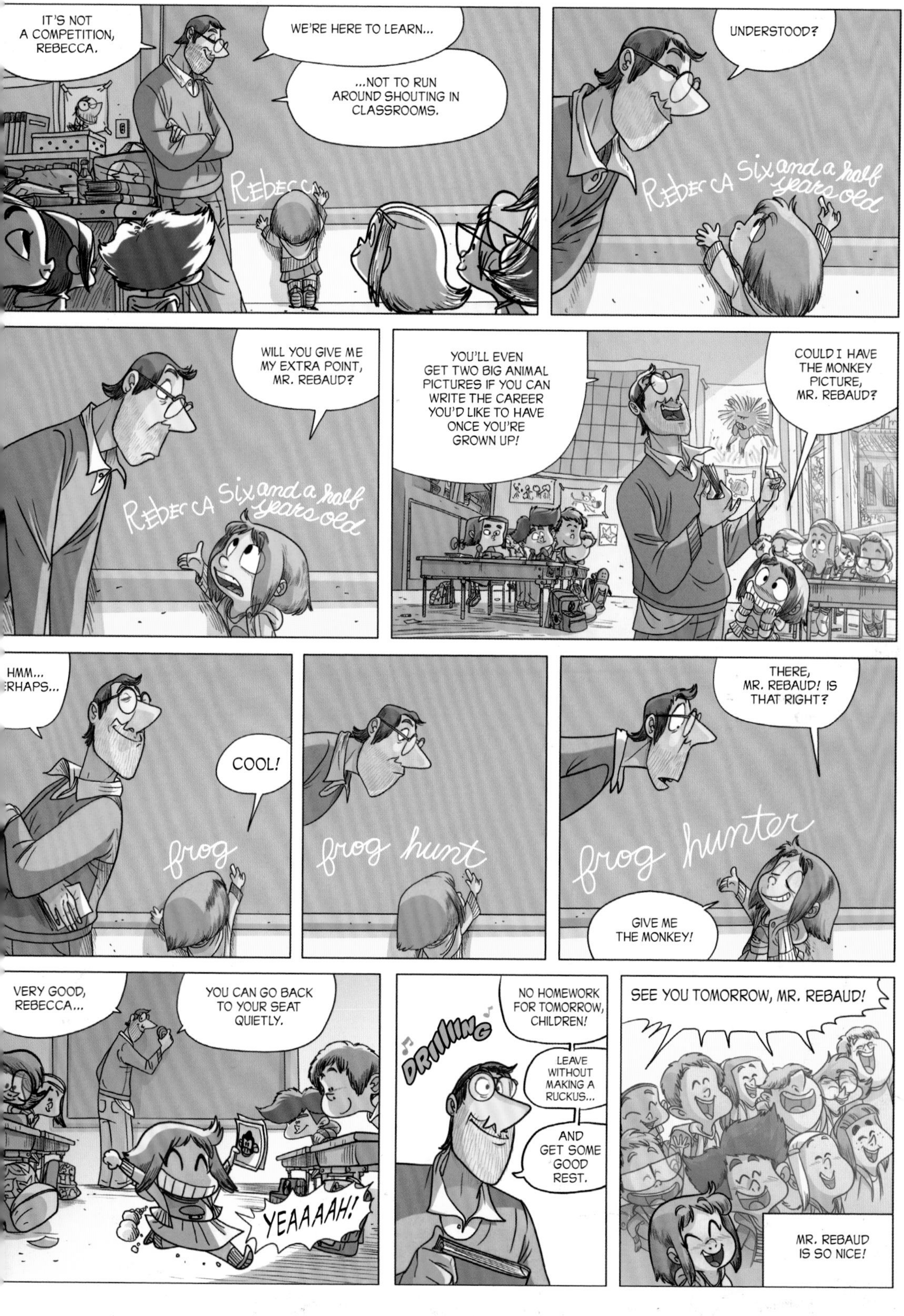

IT'S NOT A COMPETITION, REBECCA.
WE'RE HERE TO LEARN...
...NOT TO RUN AROUND SHOUTING IN CLASSROOMS.
REBECCA
UNDERSTOOD?
Rebecca Six and a half years old
WILL YOU GIVE ME MY EXTRA POINT, MR. REBAUD?
Rebecca Six and a half years old
YOU'LL EVEN GET TWO BIG ANIMAL PICTURES IF YOU CAN WRITE THE CAREER YOU'D LIKE TO HAVE ONCE YOU'RE GROWN UP!
COULD I HAVE THE MONKEY PICTURE, MR. REBAUD?
HMM... ERHAPS...
COOL!
frog
frog hunt
THERE, MR. REBAUD! IS THAT RIGHT?
frog hunter
GIVE ME THE MONKEY!
VERY GOOD, REBECCA...
YOU CAN GO BACK TO YOUR SEAT QUIETLY.
YEAAAAH!
DRIIIIING
NO HOMEWORK FOR TOMORROW, CHILDREN!
LEAVE WITHOUT MAKING A RUCKUS...
AND GET SOME GOOD REST.
SEE YOU TOMORROW, MR. REBAUD!
MR. REBAUD IS SO NICE!

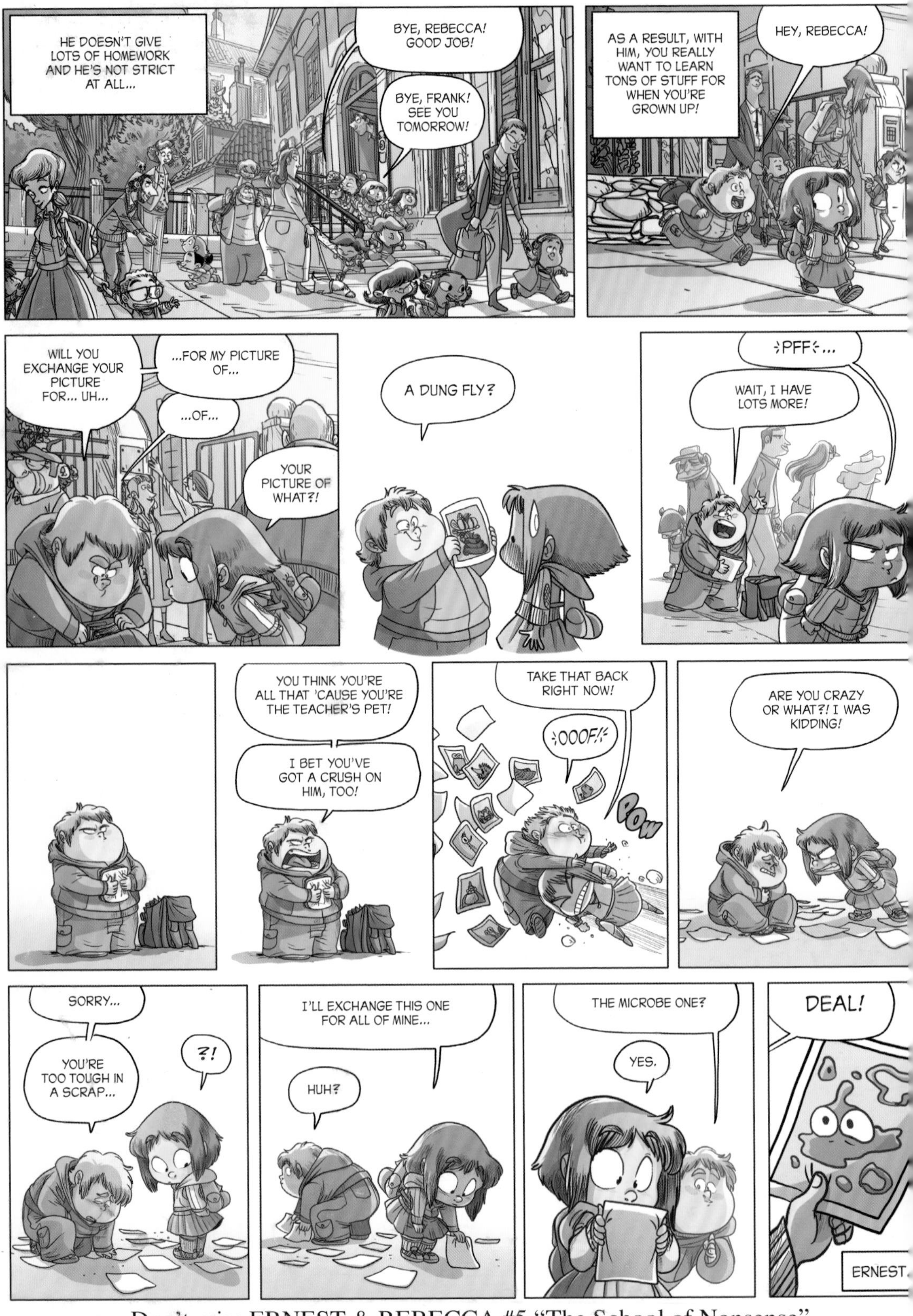

HE DOESN'T GIVE LOTS OF HOMEWORK AND HE'S NOT STRICT AT ALL...
BYE, REBECCA! GOOD JOB!
BYE, FRANK! SEE YOU TOMORROW!
AS A RESULT, WITH HIM, YOU REALLY WANT TO LEARN TONS OF STUFF FOR WHEN YOU'RE GROWN UP!
HEY, REBECCA!
WILL YOU EXCHANGE YOUR PICTURE FOR... UH...
...FOR MY PICTURE OF...
...OF...
YOUR PICTURE OF WHAT?!
A DUNG FLY?
PFF...
WAIT, I HAVE LOTS MORE!
YOU THINK YOU'RE ALL THAT 'CAUSE YOU'RE THE TEACHER'S PET!
I BET YOU'VE GOT A CRUSH ON HIM, TOO!
TAKE THAT BACK RIGHT NOW!
OOOF!
POW
ARE YOU CRAZY OR WHAT?! I WAS KIDDING!
SORRY...
YOU'RE TOO TOUGH IN A SCRAP...
?!
I'LL EXCHANGE THIS ONE FOR ALL OF MINE...
HUH?
THE MICROBE ONE?
YES.
DEAL!
ERNEST.


Don't miss ERNEST & REBECCA #5 "The School of Nonsense" available at booksellers now.